Battered Dreams

Hadena James

Acknowledgments

As always, the first thank you has to go to Mollie & Jason, who put up with the writer side of me.

A big thanks to Angela Fristoe of Covered Creatively for her excellent cover design.

For everyone that reads the series… It's my goriest book to date… Good luck! At least, I didn't leave it with a huge cliffhanger (unlike Summoned Dreams).

Also By Hadena James

The Dreams & Reality
Tortured Dreams (Book 1)
Elysium Dreams (Book 2)
Mercurial Dreams (Book 3)
Explosive Dreams (Book 4)
Cannibal Dreams (Book 5)
Butchered Dreams (Book 6)
Summoned Dreams (Book 7)
Battered Dreams (Book 8)

The Brenna Strachan Series (Urban Fantasy)
Dark Cotillion (Book 1)
Dark Illumination (Book 2)
Dark Resurrections (Book 3)
Dark Legacies (Book 4)

The Dysfunctional Chronicles
The Dysfunctional Affair (Book 1)
The Dysfunctional Valentine (Book 2)
The Dysfunctional Honeymoon (Book 3)
The Dysfunctional Proposal (Book 4)
The Dysfunctional Holiday (Book 5)

Short Story Collection
Tales to Read Before the End of the World

Screams

Sixteen-year-old Sabrina Reeves begged for her life. Tears and snot ran down her face. Her arm hung limply at her side, already shattered from warding off the first couple of blows. Sabrina was defenseless and she knew it, so she begged, trying to stop the attack.

Jess was merciless, listening to the pleading with a smile and egging it on, hoping to hear more reasons to spare Sabrina's stupid, useless life, as the bat hung menacingly.

Sabrina had not been randomly picked. Drug use and promiscuity were her only contributions to society. Sabrina couldn't even be bothered to find a minimum wage job to pay for her drugs.

"Please, Jess, don't do this!" Sabrina shouted at Jess. "I'll change! I can do it! Just give me a chance!"

Jess was growing tired of the repetitive pleas. Sabrina wasn't very imaginative. Her reasons for wanting to live were selfish and asinine. Jess brought up the bat and took a two handed grip. Sabrina screamed, raising her good arm to defend against the blow that was coming. Jess swung. The aluminum bat made a dull ringing noise as it hit Sabrina's skull, right above the ear. Blood exploded from the wound. It sprayed the bat, the wall, and the floor.

Sabrina was knocked over from the force. The world was moving even though she wasn't. The pain was consuming. Her arm hurt and tingled. Her head hurt, both on the outside and the inside. Despite the pain, she tried to convince herself it was a nightmare; one that she desperately needed to wake up from.

Jess swung the bat again, this time in a more downward motion. It caught Sabrina's shoulder. There was a cracking sound and the bat recoiled. It sent shockwaves up Jess's arms.

Sabrina was attempting to crawl away. Jess stomped on her leg and was rewarded with a wet popping noise. Sabrina screamed. The sound echoed in the small chamber. Jess's smile widened. The screams filled Jess's ears with a buzzing noise. It felt wonderful.

Jess raised the bat again. This time, it landed on the back of Sabrina's skull. Blood instantly ran from the wound. It was raised and brought down again and again and again. The bat was coated in blood. It splattered against the walls and floor. It pooled near Sabrina, who no longer screamed, but made small mewling noises.

Determined to prolong the amazing feelings, Jess stopped swinging at Sabrina's head. The bat landed body blows instead. A bone broke in Sabrina's leg with a sharp crack. A second blow hit the leg. The bone burst through the pale flesh of Sabrina's leg. Jess stared at the bone in awestruck fascination. Jess had never seen bone jutting from the skin before.

The end of the bone wept. A mixture of reddish blood and yellowish marrow leaked from the splintered end. It flowed onto the flesh, mingling with darker blood from the skin, changing the tint, before falling to the dirty floor. The floor soaked it in, as if it were water from the heavens, nourishing the brown earth.

Jess couldn't help but watch. Sabrina still made quiet, inhuman noises, but her body had stopped struggling for survival. A tremor was visible, a spasm of all her muscles, in response to the shock and pain. Sabrina's long, beautiful, auburn hair was matted and dirty. Blood made it shine in the dim lighting. Fluid that was thicker than blood, but lighter in color, dripped from the battered head. The vessels in her eyes had ruptured, turning the whites a vibrant hellish red. She drooled a mixture of blood and saliva that also soaked into the dirt.

Massive bruises were forming all over her body, proof that she was still alive, even though she shouldn't have been. The hideous purplish-black marks appeared underneath the welts. Swelling sprang up right before Jess's eyes, like magic.

The spectacle was mesmerizing. Jess let go of the bat, savoring each moment and the inhalation of a coppery tang from the blood. There was so much of it. It flowed freely from different spots. The dirt seemed to crave it almost as much as Jess.

Under the smell of blood was the smell of sweat. Sweat created from fear and pain. It stung

Jess's nostrils like vinegar, but filled some void within the brain. It was intoxicating.

The desperate, fleeting whimpers of Sabrina whispered through Jess's brain. It solicited the release of more endorphins. It kept Jess rooted to the scene, ensuring a full sensory enjoyment of the devastation she inflicted.

Jess had killed before, but never like this. The kills had always been quick, merciful. A single stab wound to the heart from behind; a skillful kill, hiding the identity of the perpetrator. Jess had done research to figure out how to kill using a single stab wound with a knife. Months had been spent practicing stabs between the wooden ribs of a dummy created specifically for that purpose.

The other kills had released the tension and stress in Jess. It allowed her to become hyper-focused on whatever project she was working on. She had aced her last exam because her ability to study was enhanced by the stress relief that killing provided to her.

Like Sabrina, Jess was sixteen and a sophomore in high school. Unlike Sabrina, she was an achiever. No goal was too lofty for her determination. Jessica Ann Blanks was an honor student, taking dual-credit classes through the University of Texas - Austin. She was president of the student council. She was captain of the volleyball team. Her older siblings were all achievers too. So were her parents. She had a role she was expected to fulfill, and she did it.

Nevertheless, it was a stressful role. It exceeded the stresses her peers felt. She had to maintain all of her achievements and balance that with an image that she also had to portray. No one could ever understand the pressure that she was under. No one could ever imagine the daily stress that she felt from maintaining all of it.

However, she didn't care if they understood, not anymore. She had found an outlet, a release. Two years earlier, she had stood by a hospital bed, watching her grandmother struggle to survive the cancer that had ravaged her body. Jess had stood there as her grandmother had taken a final gasp, her eyes turning upwards, locking with hers, and then just went blank. As she had let go, unkinking the life giving oxygen tube, she felt relief. Her stress melted away, as her grandmother's soul left its decaying husk.

It had been a mercy killing and it filled Jess with euphoria. That night, she had gone home, written her paper on the fall of the Holy Roman Empire, and slept like the dead. A full night's sleep was something she had never accomplished before. There had always been too much to do, but not that night. That night, she had been able to concentrate solely on the important things and when they were done, with her stress level reduced, she slept like never before.

Now, she needed that once in a while. The stress relief that killing brought to her. The ability to focus solely on the tasks that needed to be completed was amazing, and her sleep was blissful. The effects could last for weeks or months, at least until her next real challenge reared its head and spat its acidic demands in her face.

It was a form of control. Some teens used drugs, some were promiscuous, and some were cutters, but Jess considered all of them weak. Their stress outlets were self-destructive and provided proof that they couldn't hack it in the real world.

7

Jess was determined not to fall into the trap. She refused to let herself not be as successful as her parents and siblings. Failure was not an option.

Sabrina's eyes went blank. Her body heaved one last sigh. The room filled with the smell of urine and feces. Jess scrunched up her nose at the sudden changes. She'd been prepared for the blood and the death, but being prepared didn't mean she had to like the now soiled smells that filled her nostrils.

She'd packed water down into the cellar a day earlier. It was room temperature, making it feel chilly, as it ran over her skin. She bathed, making sure to scrub her hair as well as her body. When she was sure the blood was gone, she gathered up her clothing from the corner. They had been protected by a plastic bag. She dressed and set the bag on fire inside the now empty, but still damp bucket. It melted into a puddle at the bottom of the bucket. She waited a few moments for it to cool and then picked up the bucket. She'd toss it in a dumpster on her way home.

Exiting the cellar, she entered an old abandoned barn. The farm hadn't had a living tenant in it for at least a decade. Local losers used the barn as a party space on weekends. Graffiti decorated dilapidated walls.

It sat on a dirt road outside the limits of San Marcos, Texas. Roughly a half-hour from Austin, it was a smaller town with a population of about fifty thousand residents and one high school. Jess attended the high school, as had Sabrina.

One

Intense eyes stared at me. A question burned within them; one that I had no intention of answering. Patterson might have been my grandfather, and I might have agreed to come see him, but I wasn't here to answer all his questions.

"How are you?" He finally broke the silence that had stretched between us for almost five minutes.

"Fine. Yourself?"

"Good," Patterson smiled. "I heard your test results came back as benign."

"Yes," I told him. "As soon as we get a case, I return to active duty. They are not sure what caused it, but since it's out, I have been doing much better and almost back to my old self." I hated myself for answering the question he didn't ask.

"Eric and I have been meeting once a week with Father Bell. It was nice of you to lead him to us. He's done wonders for us."

"If I believed one psychopath could quell the anger of another, I would use it more often."

"It isn't anger he helps us with," Patterson gave a short bark of laughter that might have been a chuckle, but sounded deranged, "it's confession. It's nice to confess to someone who understands."

"One vigilante to another," I nodded.

"Exactly. I find I can talk to him and he understands me. Eric can do the same. It has been good for our souls."

"People like us do not have souls."

"Us?" Patterson cocked his head to the side.

"You, me, Eric, Bellamy Schneider, Brent Timmons, and every other monster on the planet, us. We do not have souls."

"Interesting to know you group yourself with us," Patterson said.

"I am like you, to a degree. Sometimes more like you than I want to admit. It is why I haven't visited Eric lately. I have come to realize, on a very personal level, exactly what I am."

"A cancer scare brought clarity?"

"No, the sitting around and waiting for answers after they took out a chunk of grey matter caused the revelation. Oh, I have been working my way there for a long time. I knew I had the physical characteristics of a psychopath. I knew I had urges that were hard to control, urges that wanted blood. I just wasn't willing to admit to those things. Now, I can," I paused, "and fully admit to them. It has also brought an understanding of why I'm out there and you're in here."

"Clarity is a wonderful gift. What makes it so that you walk among the population and I sit in here?"

"I trained myself to be a sociopath. I took whatever damaged mental center that controls the limited amount of emotions I can muster and ramped it up. To be blunt, I honed it, like any other skill. I turned it into something useful. I used Nyleena and my mother to do it, but I did do it. My emotions are as real as anyone else's, but they just are not the same emotions, because they are a honed skill, not a given talent." I clasped my hands in front of me. "I have also come to understand that if I can do it, almost

12

anyone should be able to do it. Malachi has to some degree, and that is why he believes we should get married. He has feelings for me. He doesn't know what they are, so he pretends they are romantic devotion. However, it works for him. His belief that I am his one true love, keeps him in the game and not out hunting game. I think you and Eric had it too. I think you both lost it, but I think you had it. Our gene pool is in need of some serious cleansing, it does create psychopaths as rain creates puddles, but it also has something in it that allows us to alter our mental state enough to change. I will never be functional. I will never feel guilt or empathy or remorse, but the other things I feel, they are real and I have to cling to those or I end up here."

"Why did you become so self-aware? That is not a trait of either sociopathy or psychopathy."

"One of my teammates told me I cry in my sleep. Since I wasn't in physical pain, the only logical conclusion was that they were caused by emotional pain. However, I didn't even weep when half my family died and my brother went to prison, so why on earth would I be feeling emotional pain? The short answer is the tumor. It stopped the flooding adrenaline that I felt. That small piece of information was the last straw. I realized that once the tumor was gone, I would go back to being me. I would not have to give up all my newfound knowledge. If I could feel with the tumor, I could feel without it."

"Do you feel?"

"Yes," I told him, "if I didn't, I would not be here."

"What do you mean?" Patterson asked.

"If I didn't feel something for you, I would not have bothered to come, but I do feel something for you. It might be love or something akin to it, or it might be something completely different, I don't know. I don't feel for you the same way I feel for my mother or Nyleena, but thinking about you evokes emotions that are not anger, nor rage, nor hatred. Therefore, it must be a fondness, much like what I feel for Eric."

"Fondness," Patterson said the word as if foreign.

"You are my grandfather, despite your flaws. Eric is my brother, despite his. I feel something for Eric. It only makes sense that I would feel something for you."

"You are always very logical, it is scary to listen to you reason out your emotions," Patterson answered. "But I will take whatever I can get. I want a relationship with you, Aislinn. That is the only reason I gave up. I could have gone down in a hail of bullets, content to know that Gertrude was dead, but I didn't. If I was dead, I wouldn't see you again and I wanted to see you again. I want to be a part of your life."

"This is how that starts," I told him. "I'm not going to pretend that seeing you fills me with joy, or makes me want to swing from the rafters, but there are worse ways to spend a Saturday afternoon. I have a question, it is a curiosity question, although it will sound work related."

"Ask away," Patterson nodded.

"About the cane, why such a heavy head and stick?"

"Have you ever been to Africa?" Patterson got a faraway look in his eyes and my response was unnecessary. "I have. I spent some time there, and I lived in an area that bordered a heavily trafficked savannah. Not trafficked by people, but by wildlife. I used to drink coffee standing outside my hut. One morning, a lion came very close to me. He was malnourished, scrawny, and desperate. For a moment, I looked like food. When he pounced at me, I did the only thing I could think to do. I hit him in the head like you would a pig. I only had a cup and my fist. I expected it to stun him. He died. He died at my feet. His hunger unsated. Later that day, the villagers where I was holed up began calling me the 'Lion Killer.' I couldn't figure out why a single blow would kill such a magnificent animal. Even malnourished and starving, he was stronger than I was, and his starvation should have made him fiercer. A few days later, I was presented with the skull. The locals had skinned it, eaten the good bits, and cleaned the skull as a trophy. Between the eyes of that skull was a hole. I didn't know it then, but lions have a very thin part on their foreheads. My blow had been enough to crush that section of skull and send chips of it into the lion's brain, killing it. Work brought me back to the US for a while and I had the cane made, it was a 'lion killer' originally, but it worked on the skulls of humans almost as well as the lions."

"Did you ever kill another lion?"

"No, I never came across another beast as pitiful as that one, and it was pitiful; rejected, dejected, prideless in more than one sense of the word. I was its last great white hope, and it fell in the attempt to conquer. That is more than most people ever manage. There was no reason to feel sorry for the creature though, it died nobly enough. "

"I knew that," I said, "about lions, I mean. They used to fight lions and bears on the frontier, as a spectator sport. I have never heard of the lion winning because the bear's natural fighting posture is to swipe at the head. In the case of a lion, that powerful swipe was all it took to end the fight."

"That is just one of the areas where you surpass me," Patterson said. "For everything I am, have been, and will be, you will always be ahead of me. You're smarter, faster, capable of a degree of compassion, and manage to be both human and monster at the same time. It makes me very proud of you."

"Compassion?" I asked.

"You feel for the lion, both in my story and in your own. Perhaps it is easier to feel for animals because they work on instincts and people do not. I don't know the answer, but I saw your face and you cared that I had killed a lion."

"He was just doing what lions do."

"Do you regret that I killed him instead of the other way around?" Patterson asked. I thought for a long time before I answered.

"No, but I can still feel like the lion was short-changed," I finally said.

Two

Sometimes, all a girl wants is a little peace and quiet. I had not received much of that in the last month. Someone snitched to my mother, Elle, and Nyleena, about them putting a hole in my skull. Xavier swears it was me. I don't believe him, but I had no evidence to the contrary, I had been on really good drugs immediately following the cranium cracking. Ativan for the panic I had experienced during surgery and then Demerol for the pain. Combined, the two drugs had removed the filter between my brain and mouth and made me forget most of it.

Thankfully, no one was holding it against me. I had said some things I would not have normally said, like telling Trevor he reminded me of a more flamboyant Elton John, or even thought of telling

Xavier that he needed to find a nice guy to settle down with. I remembered these things only after being reminded of them, as the gang had joked about them.

It turns out that my blood disorder is great at healing wounds of the flesh. They heal a little faster than average, but not as wonderful at healing wounds in the bone, they heal a little slower. The remodeling on the circle cut in my skull was about a week behind.

"How was your visit with your grandfather?" My mother asked as she scurried about the kitchen, cooking lunch. My unit was out on a hunt, tracking down a serial killer in New Jersey. I felt this was more of a lost cause than tracking down serial killers in Detroit, but that was just me. I didn't like Jersey. I'd been stuck in their airport overnight on one too many occasions.

"It was a meeting of psychopaths, the entertainment flowed like wine," I told her.

"Aislinn Cain, don't sass me."

"It's true. He told me a bullshit story about a lion. I told him I was returning to active duty as soon as possible. Psychopaths lie, that's kind of their thing. Even if you ignore my predisposition to psychopathic tendencies, I am still a sociopath and they lie. It's kind of their thing too. So, we lied to each other and managed to fill the hour and then I came home. I considered plotting world domination, but the guards were there and they would have heard."

"You are impossible." My mother threw her hands into the air. "However, he wasn't lying about the lion." She giggled at the word play. "He has the scar from it. It was during the war."

"I'm sure he lied about other stuff."

"I hope you are giving him a chance. He's not a terrible person."

"He's a serial killer."

"Well, there is that. He wouldn't win any humanitarian awards, but he's always been good to us."

"Please tell me that you have not been taking money from Patterson."

"Okay," my mother shrugged.

"Jeez, Mom."

"Sometimes, it was tight after your father died. Patterson wrote me a check every month. One of the many times he used his powers for good." She put her hand on her hip and pushed it out. I knew that stance. "You and he have that in common too. You use your powers for good."

"Mom, I love you and at this exact moment, I'm considering burying you in the backyard. Can we not talk about Patterson? I am trying to come to terms with it and establish a relationship with him. If we talk about it, I start questioning my motives."

"Fine," my mother went back into the kitchen.

"What are you cooking? You've been in there for an hour. Did you have to slaughter the cow or something?"

"Don't be ridiculous." My mother's voice came from the kitchen. "Xavier requested a low fat, low sodium diet for a while. I am making veggie taco pizza, and it takes a while to get the crust just right. It should be crispy and thin, but not cardboard."

"Why?"

"Because it's better on crispy crust."

"No, not that. Why did Xavier request a low sodium, low fat diet?"

"Because of your migraines, dear."

"Oh," I said as if that explained it all. It explained nothing. It seemed an arbitrary request and

I would have to ask Xavier about it when he wasn't shooting at bad guys.

"Why don't you work on that case thingy you were working on? It sounded interesting."

The "case thingy" was busy work. Our computer system was designed to catch patterns between multiple murders across many states. However, it had a flaw, it couldn't account for evolution or devolution. A left-handed serial killer might slit the throats of five victims, which is a very messy crime, and they would be linked as a possible case. However, if another victim shows up, eviscerated by a left-handed knife wielder, it wouldn't be linked, but it was probably the same killer. Signatures always stay the same, but killing styles can and do change. So sometimes, human eyes and logic had to go through the database to see if any kills could be linked, despite the different kill pattern.

The work varied. At times, it was interesting, other times it was dull. It was also imperfect, just because I saw a link between left-handed knife wielders, didn't mean one really existed. However, I was uniquely good at putting cases together and having them right. I understood serial killers much better than I understood the average person.

My living room had been turned into a war room for these activities. I was technically on the disabled list, assigned light duty. When you chase serial killers, there isn't much light duty work. Whether I went through the database or not, I was getting paid. This just filled the hours that I would normally spend working, and it was helpful. Our Jersey killer had been thought to have six bodies under his belt. I had identified seven more possibilities.

The Jersey killer was raping his victims before chopping off their heads. Beheadings are interesting for several reasons. First, they are hard work. Despite what the movies say, it takes work to get through the spine. A weapon can move easily through the throat, but then it hits the spine and all bets are off. Rumor says it took seven tries to behead Anne Boleyn. I believe that is probably correct. Beheading didn't get perfected until the invention of the guillotine. Second, it is really messy. It is messier than cutting a person's throat. Cutting a throat creates arterial spray from the arteries and veins that feed our brains. However, when you cut the spine, there is more arterial spray along with spinal fluid. Most of the time, the spinal fluid leaks from the wound, but once in a while it will spray out as well. Finally, there are more near beheadings than true beheadings. It takes a while to figure out where to cut to get through the spine. Beheaders usually have practice victims before the first canonical victim. In this case, four practice victims matched the pattern. Another three had their heads removed, but the killer used different tools, trying to figure out the best one. The other six were much cleaner removals, with the sixth being the best. Based on the level of skill of each beheading, it isn't difficult to go backwards and find the early work. Our killer had settled on a chainsaw, but it had taken a while to get there. He'd tried several other saws first, including a jigsaw and a Sawzall.

Having assisted the team, I was now looking for serial killers in Kansas City. There were three that we knew of, but there were probably three more that we didn't. Cities like Kansas City had a dark side that was easy to hide, most notably in the Missouri River. Few waterways had the notoriety that the Missouri River held. It was true that serial killers often dumped bodies in rivers, but they were usually found.

The Missouri was different. The current was swift with very strong undertows. The water was dark brown, because the mud and silt never really settled with the current. Large scavengers, like catfish, were plentiful and there were some very large catfish in the river. It was polluted and smelled, keeping most people from swimming in it. There was a limit on the number of fish that could be eaten from the river because of pollution, but the best cover was that it just wasn't a great place to hang out. People did it, but they weren't plentiful. This meant a body could float and still not be found for days or weeks. When bodies turned up they were scavenged, decomposed, and a lot times no longer in the Missouri, but caught in a lock and dam on the Mississippi River.

For the tracking of Kansas City serial killers, whiteboards had been dragged into my living room. My mother had a strong constitution and didn't object to the crime scene photos, or my scribblings unless

Elle and the kids were coming over, then she draped sheets over them.

I had been staring at one whiteboard for almost an hour. It bothered me, but I couldn't quite figure out why, yet. During that time, my mother had been making veggie taco pizza and humming in the kitchen, interrupting me whenever she liked. That wasn't the reason it bothered me, it just kept me from figuring out why it bothered me.

The deaths were all gunshots. A few were double homicides. Neither of these things was particularly interesting. There was a list of suspects, seventeen to be exact. That was far too many suspects, especially since they all had alibis, but it was the list I stared at.

"Pizza's done," my mother called. I got off the couch and went into the dining room. My mother had instilled in me a sense of right and wrong, and it was wrong to eat anywhere but the dining room at the table. I had a huge, hand-carved table in the garage. Patterson had made it. I refused to put it in the kitchen, but I hadn't convinced myself to get rid of it yet.

"It's good," I told my mother as I took the first bite, "but we could do takeout. I have money and it isn't that hard to get food delivered here. I cannot figure out why you insist on making all my meals."

"Because you're healing," my mother said. "You know, I was thinking of the story about Patterson and the lion. While it did happen, it might be an allegory as well."

"I thought we were not going to talk about Patterson."

"This is my last thought on the matter. Patterson was born in early August, making him a Leo. Maybe it was about conquering himself as well as the lion."

"That's it!" I jumped up from the table. "You are a genius."

"Weird," my mother muttered.

"Are you busy?" I asked Malachi as he answered the phone.

"I was sleeping. It was a long night," Malachi replied.

"Boozing or serial killers?" I asked.

"Hydrochloric acid tossed onto me by a Krokodil cook, followed by a genius trying to wash it off by hosing me down with water. I have some burns to my chest, stomach, and arms."

"Switched to hunting down drug dealers?" Krokodil was the newest, worst drug available to illegal drug users. It had earned the nickname "Flesh Eater" because Krokodil cooks used hydrochloric acid and formaldehyde in it. Using it literally rotted the flesh on the bone while the user lived to find a different spot to shoot up at.

"It was an accident," Malachi said. "We followed a suspect into what appeared to be a vacant house and found someone cooking Krokodil in the basement."

"Did you get him?"

"After he tossed the acid on me, Green put seven in his chest." Malachi was still in Detroit.

"I meant the serial killer."

"No, but we start again tomorrow. After the acid burns have gotten good scabs on them. What did you want?"

"I need you to call the Kansas City PD. I found one of their serial killers. Homicide is calling him The Shooter, sort of mimics Son of Sam kills, but I found something interesting in the case file. They had a suspect named Thad Cozie; he's the killer."

"And you know this because you are psychic?"

"No, I know this because my mother is brilliant." I answered. "So, who else did random shootings in the 1960s and 70s? The Zodiac was never captured. Thad Cozie is an anagram of The Zodiac. I think if they look a little closer, they will find some stabbings too. Also, as I stare at the murder book, I cannot help but notice that he has not left anyone alive, but I do not think it's from a lack of trying. One victim was shot once, in the arm, it just happened to hit the artery and the guy bled out. In addition, near all the shootings, they have found the same ten-digit code. They thought it was a phone number, I think it's a crude attempt to leave a cypher. Let's be honest, cyphers are tricky business and creating one of numbers that looks like a telephone number sort of ruins the effect. No one got it, because it doesn't make sense when you think of it as a phone number."

"Did you crack the cypher?" Malachi asked.

"No, I didn't even try. I think it will be gibberish, just like the cyphers of The Zodiac. That's the easy part of a cypher, it isn't hard to write down random numbers and letters and make it look like a code."

"The Zodiac contacted the papers."

"The Zodiac was forty years ago, when the papers cared. Besides, I'm not arguing that this guy is the original. I'm arguing he's a copycat and an idiot."

"Why am I calling?" Malachi asked. "You could call them."

"You didn't have a tumor removed a month ago from your brain. Even my bosses are having trouble taking me seriously. If it comes from you, they will investigate. If it comes from me, they will consider it jumping at shadows. It is possible that the strange ass name is real, but it seems unlikely given the nature of the killings and the anagram. Thad Cozie came to be on the list after an anonymous tip. I think he called in the tip. He might have been calling in to report a murder and lost his nerve, or he might be toying with the police, or he might just be an idiot.

31

I don't know. I know he has a solid alibi for two of the murders."

"Solid alibi?"

"Yes, he was playing cards both nights."

"I'm not sure how that works, Ace."

"Locard's Principle was created during a murder investigation in which the killer had set all the clocks forward an hour to create an alibi. You get some drunken 20-somethings together, change a clock, and even in the digital age, it's easy to establish an alibi."

"We have watches, cell phones, and tablets," Malachi pointed out.

"We also have strong booze in a closed off room. One of the alibi witnesses commented that they went through seven bottles of whiskey. They all passed out in the room and woke up there the next morning, both times."

"That's thin, Ace. It's not the early 1900s. It's the digital age."

"True, but when you are getting drunk with your buddies, how often do you pull out your phone and check the time?"

"I'll call them. Tell them to check him out more thoroughly."

Three

Sherlock Holmes, I was not. Despite my love for the fictional character, I wasn't much of an armchair detective. Holmes would have stared at my whiteboards and cleared up every case. I had eeked out a lead, sort of, on one. It would be chalked up as a win if I was right and Thad Cozie was a serial killer, but it still didn't make me a detective, armchair or otherwise.

My meanderings through unsolved cases had brought a gun for hire to the forefront, but judging by the files, it was already known that he was a hitman. He was very good from what I could tell. There had never been a single witness, just the unusual bullet, shot from a Luger.

The bullet didn't contain lead. They were made of tungsten carbide. No casing had ever been found, but the tungsten carbide was enough to pierce most armor. Tungsten carbide wasn't common as the primary metal in a bullet, but was usually used for the jacket, and the most unusual aspect of the bullet was the markings. The metal kept it from mushrooming or deforming, keeping the stamp pristine as it passed through the body. They were all marked "Apex."

I had a respect for contract killers. They followed the money, never asking too many questions, disappearing after the job, and reappearing only as necessary. They were colder, more calculating than the average serial killer. Yet, it still sated the monster, fulfilling its blood lust.

"That's an unusual construction for a bullet," my mother said, coming into the living room and sitting down.

"Yep," I answered. My job was technically classified, but anyone with a mother understood that sometimes, it was damn near impossible to keep it that way.

"I've seen one of those before," my mother informed me. "Armor piercing, if I remember right. It wasn't made by Apex though. Another company made it. Your father had a whole box of them. I asked why they were important and he said it would go through an elephant. I don't know if a handgun round can really go through an elephant or not, but if one could, that would be it."

"My father had a box of these?" I asked, making sure I heard her right.

"Yes, special order, super expensive. Made of some sort of composite metal. He got them for a raid shortly after you were born. Drug dealers with vests. They had tried the raid once before and lost three cops. So, your dad and a few others ordered those bullets and tried again. Didn't lose a single cop that time. Killed seven or eight high-level drug dealers. That was back when drugs were still heroin and cocaine, not this new stuff. Which reminds me, I want you to talk to the kids, especially Cassie, about this crocodile stuff."

"Is my niece in the habit of using drugs that rot her flesh?" I asked.

"I don't know, but she did get caught with something called Special K after a party. She swore someone had given it to her and she hadn't taken it, but Elle was concerned."

"Ketamine. I hope she got grounded."

"A month, and one of her punishments is to spend the day with you, listening to some of the horror stories of the people you deal with. Not the serial killers, mind you, but the prostitutes and how drugs lead to prostitution."

"Mom, I cannot lecture my niece on prostitution and its connection to drugs. It would make me a hypocrite."

"Are you a drug-addicted prostitute?"

"No," I started.

"Then you aren't a hypocrite."

"I do not think prostitution is bad. I think drugs are bad, but one does not necessarily require the other. Escorts make tons of money and work in safer environments. If we would legalize prostitution, we would not have these problems. Right now, prostitutes are victimized by the system and society; it makes sense for them to do drugs. Countries with legalized prostitution have lower drug usage among their prostitutes and lower rates of prostitution related murders, violence by johns and pimps alike, and more control over who they accept as clients."

"Aislinn," my mother gave me the look, "drugs are bad, you're a cop. Figure out something to say to her. She looks up to you."

"Why?"

"Because you are in law enforcement and can counsel her on the dangers of drugs."

"No, why does she look up to me? I'm not a good role model. I have the scars to prove it."

"Oh, that's ridiculous. Cassie is a teenager. She thinks the scars are cool. She thinks it's cool that you chase serial killers, and you're her aunt. While other kids have aunts who are postwomen and grocery store clerks, her aunt is a real life boogeyman. Your recent health scare and dealings in Detroit made you just that much more cool, because you took down several serial killers while suffering from a brain tumor. Like it or not, you are a role model to girls all over the world. Your niece isn't excluded."

"I repeat, I am not a good..."

"Pish," my mother waved her hand at me, "you hunt down bad guys, proving to little girls that they don't have to be victims. They can fight back. They have a voice. They are not just prey for the predators. They are people and they can survive anything thrown at them."

"That is a terrible idea. Next, you'll be wanting me to go to career day."

"You may think it's a terrible idea, but it isn't. You refused to be a victim as a child. You refuse to be a victim now. Millions of little girls are growing up, watching you kick butt on television news programs and are being inspired to grow up and take care of themselves. I couldn't be prouder of you. Cassie is coming this afternoon. I expect sheets over these boards unless you can fill them with gruesome photos of crocodile users."

"Krokodil, Mom, it's called Krokodil."

"Well, can you fill a board with those photos?"

"I could," I admitted, "but does she need that sort of visual aid? Krokodil is bad."

"If it was pot, I wouldn't have asked you to talk to her," my mother huffed off. Obviously, pot was more tolerable than Krokodil and Special K. In truth, I didn't know much about drugs. I knew about the chemical makeup. I knew that Krokodil was a sure way to die, but I had never even smoked pot. I knew what I was going to be spending the afternoon doing.

Cassie showed up on schedule. Elle could make the trains run on time. She wasn't evil, just efficient when it came to the time management of herself and her children. All my whiteboards were covered. My mother busied herself in my pitiful backyard, insisting on planting spring flowers that would die because I would forget about them.

"If I had taken the drugs, Mom wouldn't have found them," Cassie started talking before she had even sat down. "I know better than to take that crap. We are a family with a history of mental instability. If I start snorting cocaine or injecting heroin or popping Special K and XTC, there's a good chance I will go off the deep end. I love you, Aunt Ace, but I don't want to be like you. I feel bad for you, going through life without any real happiness or the ability to fall in love."

"Smart girl," I said. "I am not going to lecture you on the dangers of drugs. I am going to talk to you about the two big ones; meth and Krokodil."

"I had a class, we talked about meth. It makes your teeth fall out, your skin dry out, and your brain freak out. I would never do that."

"What do you know about Krokodil?"

"I've never heard of it."

"Krokodil itself is bad, but it's just a narcotic. However, it's how they make Krokodil that I want you to be aware of. Not because I think you are stupid enough to use it, but because if you know the signs, you can report anyone that uses it. This is serious, Cassie, Krokodil hasn't hit the streets as heavy as meth or cocaine, but if it does, we'll be in the midst of an epidemic. Krokodil is toxic when cooked on the streets. It doesn't matter how it enters the body, there are some serious chemicals that you don't want in it. They cause your skin to die, turning it black. It may ooze, like a spider bite from a Black Widow or Brown Recluse, but in a much larger section. Necrosis can cause amputations, serious infections, and death. Your bones can start rotting. That's painful and makes them break. It also decreases your white and red blood cell counts because the marrow can't make them anymore. You become prone to infections of the blood, bone, skin, and organs. Most of the infections are fatal. It causes blood clots too. If your friends start showing up with patches of necrotized skin, you need to tell someone."

"How will I know?"

"You'll know. If your friend comes in one day and they smell like rotting flesh, and their arm is turning black, it's obvious they are on this stuff. Krokodil is almost always fatal in one way or another."

"Ok, as a sixteen year old girl, living in Kansas City, should I be more concerned about Krokodil or serial killers?" The girl looked at me in earnest.

"Honestly, date rape is probably your biggest fear at the moment. We don't have any predators of teen girls at the moment. Krokodil is horrible, but it is concentrated in areas where the Russian Mob is the highest. If you are going to a party, take your own drinks. Watch for the signs of being drugged; they are hard to recognize, but it's like mixing extra strength Benadryl with large amounts of alcohol. You'll feel sleepy, confused, and uncoordinated. Immediately call someone if you feel this way. Never leave your group of friends at a party. If they ditch you, go home."

"I know about GHB," Cassie said.

"Oh, it isn't just GHB anymore, Cass. If my work with SCTU has taught me anything, it's that drugging people is easier than you think. I have seen killers snatch their victims using Benadryl and whiskey. Even extra strength Tylenol or Excedrin Migraine can be mixed with stuff to make a person unconscious. Add in a little X and they become even easier to control. Or Special K. Did a boy give you the Special K?"

"Yeah," Cassie said.

"May I have his name? I can't bust him for the drugs, but I would like to talk to him."

"I don't know."

"Is he your friend?"

"Well, sort of."

"Cassie, you were drinking alcohol at a party. He gave you Special K, and you take medicine for an anxiety disorder. Does he know this?"

"Yeah, he knows I'm on meds for anxiety."

"Then either he's an idiot, or he is not even sort of your friend. Ketamine is a tranquilizer. If mixed with your regular anxiety meds, it could have killed you. It most certainly would have incapacitated you. You would have no memory of the night, which is how I know you did not take it." I thought for a moment. "I don't care that you were drinking. You're a teen, teens drink. I would prefer you do it with supervision since you are so sensitive to meds and have to take barbiturates instead of anti-depression medications. Even alcohol and barbiturates can kill you in the right doses. Adding a strong tranquilizer like Ketamine would be horrendous. They use it to knock out horses and large livestock, not just people. I have even heard of it being used on elephants to prep them for surgery. Ketamine is not something to screw around with."

Cassie stared at her hands for a few minutes. Her teeth chewed on her bottom lip. Like me, Cassie's brain chemistry made some drugs worse than they should be. The poor girl had tried to kill herself on seven different occasions because of antidepressants, and while benzodiazepines worked well for me, helping me sleep from time to time, they made her anxiety worse. Barbiturates, however controversial, were about the only thing left for her.

The dosage was small, but it was still a barbiturate. Xavier helped monitor her when she was at my house. I worried about her.

"Ok," Cassie finally said, looking up at me with large round eyes, "I'll tell you."

She didn't tell me, she wrote it down. She also wrote down the date of the party, everyone she remembered being there and the boy's parents' names. I took the sheet, folded it up, and put it in my pocket.

"I will not tell your grandmother or mother about this information. I'm sure they will find out though."

"I'll tell them," Cassie sighed.

"I have a gift for you, but you are only to use it in cases of extreme emergencies," I handed her a box. Inside was a small stun gun that I had been given to test out. I hadn't liked it, it didn't work well on psychopaths, but it would drop a teenage boy. "Here's the deal. Do not hit them in the chest with it, or the neck like you see in the movies. Hit them in the crotch. You'd be amazed at how effective that is."

"So, if someone is trying to rape me, you want me to stun gun their crotch?"

"Yep," I answered. "They lose their erection, immediately ejaculate, and collapse into a crying ball because of the pain. I have used the technique on naked serial killers, but with my Taser. It is more effective than the chest and less likely to cause a heart attack or stroke. It's also not legal for you to have it. If you get caught with it, send the police in my direction. I can smooth that over."

Four

The house in front of me was a two-story brick mansion. There was no other word to describe the sprawling wings and tall windows on the front, like giant staring eyes. I grabbed my wallet, my badge, and my US Marshals jacket. I didn't care about class, as I was comfortable in my jeans and T-shirt. I cared about appearing to be authoritative. It was my intention to scare the boy and his incredibly wealthy parents into wetting themselves, and if I could get the kid grounded for the rest of his natural teenage life, that would be a bonus.

The large front door opened before I could ring the doorbell or knock. A tall, leggy brunette with perfectly manicured nails and sparkly teeth stood in front of me. She seemed concerned with my appearance on her doorstep, as if my jeans and

Charger might tarnish their reputation with their neighbors.

"May I help you?" She asked.

"US Marshal Aislinn Cain," I answered. "I'm here to speak to the parents of Chris Chadwick."

"I'm Mrs. Chadwick. May I ask what this is about?"

"Mrs. Chadwick, are you aware that three weeks ago, your son held a party at this house?"

"I am aware that our sons had a few friends over while my husband and I were in Tampa. I would hardly call it a party."

"According to the security agents that patrol your neighborhood, there were over a hundred teenagers present. They also noted that several people were seen holding alcoholic beverages. They took pictures, and I have them in my possession. Would you like to see them?"

"Maybe you should come in," Mrs. Chadwick stepped out of the doorway. Her heels clicked against the floor. "Chris, Ryan, Peter, could you all join me in the living room, please?"

Cranky, sleep deprived twin teens entered the living room first. I had my badge now attached to my jacket. One flopped onto the couch; the other paled a little and sat down with less gusto. I was guessing I knew which one was Chris.

"Darlene, I'm very busy," Peter Chadwick stopped talking and stared at me. It was unlikely this family got many visits from the police, let alone a US Marshal. It was worth a stare or two.

"Mr. Chadwick?" I asked.

"Doctor actually," he corrected me.

"Oh, I apologize. US Marshal Aislinn Cain, I'm following up on a party that was held here three weeks ago by at least one of your sons."

"Why are the US Marshals following up on a party?" He asked.

"The DEA is busy today," I responded. His face looked shocked. He sat down, as did his wife. "I'm sure you are aware that your neighborhood is routinely patrolled by a private security firm, yes?"

"Of course, it is part of our neighborhood fees," Mrs. Chadwick told me.

"Those security agents received multiple noise complaints and began taking photos and videos of the party when they met with resistance. It is my understanding they asked on two occasions for the party to break up, but it continued. At that time, they began documenting the event. The documentation shows underage drinking, nude teenagers running through the yard, including one of your sons, however, the part that concerns us the most is that after the party, the security guards stopped a car. They asked the driver to take a sobriety test, which they passed. After that, they asked to search the vehicle and were given permission. One of the teenagers in the car, a fifteen-year-old girl, had a drug called Special K on her. In small doses, Ketamine is an effective sedative, but in this dosage, it would have knocked the girl out and possibly killed her. When questioned, she informed the security agents that she was given the pill by Chris Chadwick, who hosted the party."

"Why would my son have drugs?" Mrs. Chadwick asked, as Dr. Chadwick looked even grimmer. I was pretty sure someone was going to get a serious punishment when I left.

"I'm not sure. What I do know is that Dr. Chadwick's work with the Kansas City Zoo makes us fairly certain that he was the original source of the Ketamine. The dosage is just about perfect for a large cat, such as a tiger or lion. Have you recently needed to operate on such an animal, Dr. Chadwick? Do you keep Ketamine in your home?"

"Yes," Dr. Chadwick hung his head. The paler twin paled even more, looking downright ill. "I keep Ketamine at the house because I also work with large livestock. The dosage for a large cat and a hog are the same. I keep it locked in my office in case I need to respond to an emergency with a hog."

"Do you know how many tablets you have in your possession?"

"I have twenty tablets and seven vials of liquid Ketamine."

"Could you go count those tablets and provide proof of distribution?"

"Now you are accusing my husband of distributing the drugs?" Mrs. Chadwick was on the verge of hysteria.

"No, I believe one or both of your sons, broke into the storage area where your husband keeps his Ketamine and took at least one tablet out, which was then passed on to a fifteen year old girl."

"Our sons wouldn't do such a thing," Mrs. Chadwick huffed, trying to pull herself together.

"Maybe this girl broke into the cabinet and took them herself."

"The girl in question requires other medications and is aware that mixing a strong sedative like Ketamine with her other medications would result in death. However, I can easily have someone come fingerprint and DNA swab the cabinet to verify that it wasn't her." I pulled out my phone and abused my power as a US Marshal working with the SCTU.

"There are eleven pills missing," Dr. Chadwick said as he came back into the living room, "and it isn't the first time it has happened. I blamed my nephew the first time, because he was a recovering addict. I sent him back to rehab. Did I make a mistake?" This last bit wasn't directed at me, so I stayed quiet. Both boys were obviously mute too. Their silence stretched on for ages.

"Are you going to arrest them?" Mrs. Chadwick suddenly stood up.

"It is not my intention," I told her.

"Then get out of my house," she pointed towards the door.

"Thank you for your time. I will pass this information along to the local police as well as the DEA. You have a great rest of the day." I let myself out. As I left, I made sure to rev the engine of my car. I also called the tech and told them to turn around and work on real cases. I had hoped they would let me fingerprint and DNA swab so that I could point the finger directly at their sniveling spoiled brats. However, I did call Agent Franklin with the DEA. A doctor who mishandles medications was always interesting. For all the doc knew, his kids could be dealing Ketamine and cooking the liquid into a powder for snorting or smoking. I didn't know if Ketamine actually worked that way, but most liquids could be powdered and snorted or smoked.

In reality, I expected Franklin to blow me off. So, my niece had been given a single tablet of Ketamine, no biggie. There were much worse drugs available to teenagers and there was the real possibility that Krokodil would be hitting the urban centers soon.

He didn't though. He took all the information. His fingers could be heard typing on a kcyboard as I talked. Then promised to be in touch.

This meant something. Somehow, I had managed to create a rapport with a DEA agent. It was a nice change from other law enforcement officials who whispered about our mental health and choice of jobs.

My intention was to stare at the "Apex" bullets some more. They were custom jobs. There couldn't be that many ammunition manufacturers that could build them. Of course, someone had thought of that before and it had gotten him or her nowhere.

"Hey, Cain," the gate attendant, Jimmy, said as I stopped to get buzzed in, "I was just about to send someone to your place. You have a package."

"A package?" I asked. I didn't receive a lot of packages and when I did, they usually bled. "Is it something dead?"

"Quite the opposite," Jimmy buzzed the gate and I pulled my car through it. Once the gate was closed, I got out of the car and walked to the guard shack. Jimmy was holding a leash. Attached to the leash was a dog, a cute dog with a curled tail, big paws, and tiny legs.

"You're kidding, right?"

"Nope, he was delivered about twenty minutes ago. The paperwork says he's a rescue dog. They know he is part Akita, but not the other stuff." Jimmy handed me the paperwork to sign.

"Akitas are big dogs, and this isn't that big of a dog."

"You've never had a dog before, have you?"

"Not that I remember."

"Dogs start out as puppies. Yours is about five months old."

"What am I going to do with a dog?" I asked no one.

"Feed it, play with it, start staying in pet friendly hotels, let it poop in Blake's yard," Jimmy offered suggestions.

I took the paperwork and examined it to find out who had sent me a dog. I had expected it to be a giant joke at my expense from Xavier, or a companion from Lucas and Trevor. Instead, the name at the bottom of the form was my mother's.

Putting the puppy in the car, I told the guards thanks while silently wondering if my mother had lost her damn mind. To give me a puppy was beyond unexplainable. I was never home and I didn't know what to do with it when I was.

"Mom!" I shouted as I walked into the house, puppy still on its leash.

"Oh good, he arrived," she squealed. "Isn't he just the cutest thing ever?"

"Well, he's cuter than the grandkids that you thought were adorable and I thought looked like tiny aliens. Why did you get me a puppy? I'm never home. How am I supposed to take care of him?"

"I didn't get you a puppy," she blinked at me. "I got us a puppy. A little unconditional love could go a long way around here. It'll be good for both of us."

"Us? I'm confused by the us? Are we time sharing the dog?"

"You don't remember, do you?"

"Remember what?"

"I'm moving in here. With Patterson in jail, my getting older, and you being notorious, you decided I should come live with you," my mother told me. "Besides, you need someone to help take care of you when you are home. You're always bruised, broken, burnt, and beat up."

"That's a lot of 'B' words. Do you have it in writing that I made this decision?"

"I do. We had a contract drawn up," my mother handed me some paperwork. The first clause was that we got a puppy. I checked the last page. It was definitely my signature at the bottom. What the hell had the drugs done to me?

Home

The top of the paper said "A: excellent work!"
It was excellent work. Jess had poured herself into
the paper and been rewarded appropriately. Of
course, she had known that she would be. It was rare
for her to get anything less than an A. Once in a great
while, she scored an A-, but she always did extra
work to keep it from hurting her grades.

"Hey!" Her best friend, Becky Childs, called
to her from down the hall. "Are you going this
weekend?" Matt Dover was hosting a party at his
house on Saturday, while his parents visited his
grandmother in Colorado. Becky had the hots for
Matt. Matt didn't seem to reciprocate, but that didn't
stop Becky from trying.

"I don't know yet," Jess answered. She slung
her book bag over her shoulder and sized up her

friend again. Becky was attractive. Black hair with just a hint of purple, fair skin that didn't belong to her Spanish heritage, and absolutely zero acne. Her eyes were a rich brown, like coffee with a dollop of cream. Jess still hadn't figured out why Matt didn't like Becky. She had offered to find out, but Becky refused to let Jess intervene.

"Even you deserve a night of fun and booze," Becky chided her. "One night won't kill you or your status as future valedictorian."

"You're right," Jess sighed. "Maybe Simon will be there. We should go shopping before the party. Got plans this afternoon?"

"Well, I'm supposed to be studying, but I could use a new outfit for the party," Becky laughed. "Want to meet around six tonight? I have to make sure the brats get home." Becky had two younger sisters. Her mother worked in Austin and her dad worked in San Antonio, so she was responsible for making sure her sisters made it home and started their homework.

The house was quiet when Jess got home. Her parents were both at work and she didn't have any younger siblings. It didn't take long for her to get settled on the couch and get Netflix turned on. She checked her social media while watching a rerun of *Gossip Girl*.

Her mother, Carly, surprised her by walking through the door before the episode was even half over. Carly looked grim. Her eyes were red rimmed. The skin around her upper lip was red, a sign she'd been chewing on it, a terrible habit that manifested when Carly Blanks was very upset.

"Mom, what's wrong?" Jess asked, concerned. Her mother was a pediatrician. It was rare for the doctor to show raw emotion as she was right now.

"We need to talk, Jessie," Carly put down her shoulder bag. She hadn't brought home any files or paperwork. That was really unusual too. Jess's stomach tightened. "You know the boy, Nathan, that went missing a few months ago, they found him. They found him and others today, in a well, near the Hawthornes' place."

"Nathan?" Jess searched her memory. She vaguely remembered him. He was a skateboarder that had been in her English class. Jess had lured him out to the Hawthorne farm using the promise of easy sex, and then she'd stabbed him in the back and tossed him in the well with four other bodies. His car and skateboard had been found on a dirt road on the other side of town. Jess wondered how they had found her previous dumping grounds. The Hawthornes hadn't used that well as long as she'd been alive. It was too far from the house for the scent to give it away and she'd dumped in a bunch of lye from the Hawthornes' soap making stockpiles.

"He was in your class, you mentioned his disappearance at the beginning of the year," Carly told her. Jess studied her face for a moment, took note of the shock and horror, and attempted to mimic it as she sat down.

"I remember. He's dead? Who else did they find?"

"They haven't released any other names. I'm not sure they know yet. Nathan wasn't as badly decomposed as the others."

That was good information. The lye must need to be layered. She'd done that with the first three bodies, but had gotten lazy with Nathan. Angela Schmidt had gone in after Nathan and she'd taken the time to dump the lye on her. Angela's body must have protected Nathan's from the caustic material and slowed decomposition.

Of course, now she had changed dumping grounds to the abandoned ranch. She needed something to put on the bodies she planned to put there. Also, if she was going to continue with her new method, she would have to learn to kill them somewhere else and then put them in the cellar. That would get tiring. Volleyball kept her body strong, but dead bodies were heavy. There was no way to target victims smaller than her and even if she did, they would be heavy if she had to move them very far.

Her mother was talking to her about the nature of death and about how shocking it was to lose a classmate to violence. Jess was only half listening. She'd blame her reaction on shock if anyone asked too many questions. Killing someone in the cellar was risky, but the entrance was well hidden and the ceiling had been thick. It was more like a fallout shelter than a cellar. However, if she moved her activity to the barn, the risk intensified exponentially. Kids used the barn to smoke pot and throw parties.

Of course, there were other buildings on the property, and some were more dilapidated than others, but she could start using one of these buildings for her purposes. She would have to do more reconnaissance on the area.

"Honey, are you alright?" Carly touched Jess's hand, making Jess jump.

"Yeah, no, I don't know, Mom. I didn't know Nathan, but it's shocking to find out someone your own age has been murdered." Jess frowned. "These are supposed to be some of the best years of our lives and to be snuffed out so uncaringly during that time seems surreal."

"If you want to talk, you can. I'm here, your dad will be available and I'm sure they will make the school counselor available. We can go to Austin and you can see someone privately. You've always been unsure about death, since you watched your grandmother pass away. There's no shame in seeking a professional to help you sort out your feelings."

"Thanks, Mom, but I'm okay, I just need to process this information. Do you think it's safe to go out? I'm supposed to meet Becky tonight to go to the mall."

"Why wouldn't it be?" Carly asked.

"Well, they did find five people in a well. I don't think they were all dropped in by different people," Jess said pointedly.

"As long as you two stick together, I'm sure you will be fine. Does this trip to the mall have anything to do with Matt's party this weekend?"

"It does and how did you know?" Jess smiled at her mother.

"I hear things. Go get a new outfit, dear, and have some fun. Maybe hanging out with Becky will help you process," Carly smiled.

Five

Some people hated flying, others loved it; I was somewhere in the middle. It wasn't the worst thing on the planet, but it wasn't the greatest either. My ears didn't always pop as they should. The drone of the plane's engines caused a small headache, and even though I was the only passenger on the small, private jet, I couldn't fall asleep. This was partly because I had trouble sleeping on planes and partly because I had just finished reading a book on crystal skulls.

Keeping an open mind was very important to me. My best guy friend believed that cattle mutilations were either secret government projects, or aliens in search of food. My best girlfriend believed that the space race was about creating a super weapon that would blow up any asteroids, intent on recreating the extinction event that wiped out the dinosaurs.

However, even I wasn't buying the legend of the Skull of Doom. It was so farfetched that I was willing to believe aliens carved it and accidentally dropped it on one of their animal mutilation food foraging trips, while they watched the space around earth to keep another extinction level asteroid from happening. It was absolutely not a hand carved Mayan artifact found in Belize in 1927, as the legend claimed.

Thankfully, the plane was beginning its descent. I was landing in Austin, Texas, but it might as well have been the dark side of the moon. I knew nothing about Austin or Texas. I had never had a desire to visit the state. The cartels dominated most of the border towns and I had no intention of tangling with the cartels. Texas had its own elite law enforcement; the Texas Rangers, and they didn't invite the federals in very often.

The team was already on the ground in a town called San Marcos. We had, in fact, been invited by the Texas Rangers to deal with a serial killer. They'd only found five bodies, which didn't seem that high, but since Texas was currently in a border war with the cartels, they were really hoping we'd swoop in, claim it was the cartel, and go on our merry way. From what Gabriel had said after telling me I was cleared for duty, it was not going to be the case.

We landed at a small airfield outside the city limits. Theoretically, I was going to have an escort to San Marcos, but as I debarked the plane, I didn't see one. There was a small lobby area and I made my way to it. It was already getting warm in Texas and I saw no reason to stand in the heat and wait for my ride.

There was a small cafeteria, a kiosk selling tourist crap, a waiting area with chairs, and a security station manned by two guards. No one looked at me as I wandered in from the tarmac. Everyone was glued to his or her electronic devices. It was amazing how often technology actually disconnected us from the world. My iPhone was securely shoved in my back pocket. Whether it was charged or not, I had it.

I liked the benefits of technology, but I didn't have to have the latest and greatest of anything. Most of my electronic devices became gaming and book reading equipment after about a week. Sure, I could make and receive phone calls, but it was the only phone feature I used. I didn't even have social media profiles. My niece, Cassie, kept trying to get me to download something called Snapchat, but I hadn't because I wasn't sure I'd be able to figure out how to use it.

A shirt caught my attention. It was tie-dyed and in bold, glittery letters, said "Keep Austin Weird." I had no idea what that meant, but once I had seen the phrase, it began jumping out at me from other items. It was plastered on coffee mugs, ink pens, postcards, and even a small teddy bear. From what I had seen of Austin, the only thing weird was this phrase bombarding me from kitsch souvenirs.

"Marshal Cain?" A woman's voice made me turn around. "Ranger Stephanie LaComb; I apologize for the wait. There was a big flap this morning that I was trying to deal with."

"I understand." Ranger LaComb had a strong accent. She was petite, both shorter and lighter than I was, blond and pretty. The pantsuit she wore made her appear dainty. Her blond hair was long and arranged into a thick braid that ran to the middle of her back. If my hair would have been capable of staying in a braid, I would have considered letting it grow long. It wouldn't, too fine to stay in such an intricate fashion. I was trying not to make snap judgments, however, Ranger LaComb didn't impress me at first sight. I had learned this meant little, some small, dainty women were actually badasses, and she could be one of those. After all, she was a Texas Ranger.

"There are reporters out front, so we'll go out the back, if you don't mind." LaComb began leading the way to a door marked "Authorized Personnel Only" that had a keypad.

"What sort of flap happened last night?" I asked.

"A bunch of local stoners from the college swear they saw a UFO abduct a girl," LaComb smiled. "It is Austin."

"Is there a missing girl?" I asked.

"Around here, there are lots of missing girls. It's a college town. It has crime like any place else and it has deserters. Kids who run home to mommy and daddy and don't tell anyone, or run off with their girlfriends or boyfriends and don't tell anyone. In this case, the girl was here at the airport, and the witnesses were smoking weed laced with LSD when a bright light landed, aliens got out and abducted her, then it took off again. We believe she got on a private jet and are attempting to follow up with her parents, but the idiots went to the press before us, so it's a feeding frenzy."

"Gotcha. That's why I prefer serial killers, there usually aren't witnesses left to describe aliens." I stopped as a word floated through my head. My witnesses never described aliens, but they did see monsters. Gabriel had seen a wendigo when he had been young. It had attacked a classmate, broke the kid's leg and began sucking on the splintered bone. The kid died of infection and the monster got away. Gabriel was convinced it was a wendigo. The terrified look on his face ensured I didn't argue that he had simply replaced the face of a real person with the legendary creature because of shock when he finally told me the story.

"That's an odd thing to say," LaComb pushed through the door and we entered a quiet hallway.

"Well, if it turns out to be a missing person, your only lead flies around in a saucer shaped disk with a bright light."

"I see your point." We exited the airport terminal. A black truck with tinted windows and a light bar was running near a hanger. I tossed my bags into the backseat and climbed into the front, thankful for the running boards. "So how long will it take to make a determination if we have a serial killer in San Marcos or not?"

"My presence is an indication that the distinction has already been made and San Marcos has one. One who, by all accounts, is rather tame. The killer is using a single stab wound, indicating that they enjoy the finality of it, not the brutality of it."

"Killing is killing."

"People kill for different reasons. Some like the torture of the death. Some like the death itself. I'm not a shrink, so I can't tell you why there's a difference, but I can tell you there is one. This one should be relatively easy to catch. They may even consider it mercy killing. My file says they are still working to identify all the bodies."

"Yeah, it appears the killer put lye in the well." Ranger LaComb maneuvered away from the airport via an access road. "So, there is no way this is the cartels?"

"Nope, cartels like to make statements and this is too far north for a border war. Everything I have seen says serial killer. If my boss didn't agree, I would not have been on a private flight this morning on my way to Texas." I stared out the window and watched the city of Austin disappear.

The tires hummed on the road, still wearing out the newness of the treads. Ranger LaComb's radio was on low, creating a constant murmur, reminding me of Charlie Brown's teacher. The air conditioner was too high, causing goosebumps, despite the long sleeves that covered my arms. The landscape rolled by without holding my interest. The Skull of Doom still filled my primary thoughts. Unfortunately, if it was a fake, there was a good chance all the others were too. That was mildly depressing in the grand scheme of things. A hand carved, ancient crystal skull would have been a feat of human engineering. As a historian, it felt like a blow to the early accomplishments of mankind.

Of course, our early roots had built amazing pyramids and practiced human sacrifice. It didn't seem like we had progressed much in the millennia since then. We were still practicing human sacrifice and building giant buildings. Technology had changed, styles of construction had changed, but humans really hadn't.

Six

The morgue smelled of decomposition and astringent. This was standard for morgues. Xavier's smile was not. He was happy to have me back in my usual place, sitting in the morgue, offering him ideas.

Two of the victims were male, three were female, and none were adults. Other than that, they hadn't come up with any useful information. One victim was identifiable, Nathan Jones, a local high school student who preferred skateboarding to classrooms. He'd gone missing in October. He was a suspected runaway, based on his home life. The report called it "unhappy."

I thought that was an understatement. Before becoming a skateboarding school skipper, he had been a punching bag for his father. He'd run away several times in the past, always ending up at his aunt's house. His aunt had filed several reports of abuse against her brother, but Nick's mother always told a different story.

Obviously, the teen hadn't caught a break and escaped to live in better places. I wanted to talk to the father, but I doubted he was the serial killer. It was unusual for serial killers to behave that way towards their own families. They liked to kill and they couldn't do that if they were in jail for beating the shit out of their wives and children. Accidentally killing their own offspring was a good way to get caught.

There was another child in the house. What I really wanted to do was inspire the father to leave that one alone. I had plenty of weapons to help if I couldn't do it with a stern talking.

"You are sneering." Xavier interrupted my reading.

"Have we talked to the father?"

"No, Gabriel was waiting for you."

"He rocks. I'll have to buy him a thank you gift."

"Well, not only are none of them adults, all are roughly the same age. I'd put them at fifteen to seventeen."

"So, not just a serial killer, but one that preys on teenagers. At least they aren't preying on children."

"I can't determine how long they have been in the well. The lye and water accelerated decomp. We'll have to do comparisons to dental x-rays and if that doesn't work, facial reconstructions."

"One is definitely a local," I told him. "The others probably are too. Especially considering they were found locally. You'd think they would have been searching for a body dump earlier."

"Do you have any idea how many people go missing every year?" Xavier asked.

"Roughly a million people a year, about seventy percent are under the age of eighteen, and ninety percent will either not be found or will be found dead."

"So in a town of fifty thousand people, five missing teenagers in the space of an unknown number of years, doesn't really point to a serial killer." Xavier reminded me. "They probably average twenty missing children a year plus a handful of adults. It really isn't their fault they didn't notice a low-volume serial killer."

"If this victim was high risk, the others probably were too. It just seems like someone should be responsible."

"Other than the killer?"

"Yes," I answered.

"Who should we hold accountable?"

"The parents," I answered. "If they had done their jobs, their children wouldn't have been high risk."

"It's nice to have you back. That simplistic logic that comes across as harsh to anyone that doesn't know you."

"I think that's supposed to be a compliment."

"It is," Xavier looked at the bodies still on the table. "Want to take a look and see if I missed anything?"

"I could, but I'm sure you didn't miss anything." I got off the counter where I had been seated and began walking around the bodies. Two of them were mostly skeletons, two others were heavily decomposed, and the final was almost perfect, like it had been preserved somehow. The eyes had clouded over, removing most of their color. The skin had become waxy looking. It didn't look like it was about to sit up, but it was very obviously a human being.

As a general rule, I do not touch dead bodies. That's Xavier's job. I didn't have any instinct to touch this one either. I didn't even want to look at it. Something in the lifeless face or sightless eyes bothered me. Maybe I wasn't as healed as I thought.

The others didn't raise my hackles. They were just bodies like I had seen dozens of times before. Some connective tissues and flesh remained, but their facial features were gone. Exposed skull, stained an orangish color, was visible through some patches of matted hair.

"Well?" Xavier asked, as I stopped to look at the exposed skull of one of the victims.

"Not very impressive," I answered.

"Lucas said it's about the act of killing and the transition of life to death and not about the need to create violence."

"Mercy killings, maybe," I sighed. I had already had that thought and vocalized it, but it was different vocalizing it to Xavier. The very words sounded different.

"It would explain the lack of violence. The stab wound is very precise, entering between the ribs at the back and penetrating the heart. There are no hesitation marks. It would take a very adept knowledge of anatomy to be able to slide it through the ribs like it is."

"Doctor? Nurse? That fits with a mercy killer."

"Yes, but I have something I want to show you," he rolled the body of Nathan Jones over. There was a bruise where the hilt had hit the skin at the time of death. Next to the hilt bruise was another mark. It was almost perfectly round. In the center of the circle was another shape, but less defined. "Strange, right?"

"I'd guess it's a ring, but it would be in the wrong position if someone was stabbing someone else," I told him.

"Those were my thoughts. So, I looked a little closer," he pulled up a photo on a computer. The circle magnified, became identifiable, it was a button. Our killer wore gloves.

"And Lucas's take?"

"He says it is just another reminder that the killer is mature," he said.

"You disagree?"

"I'm not sure," Xavier said.

"Why would you think they were young?" I pressed.

"A gut feeling. The knife wound. Victim four was preserved, and the others were not, because the killer didn't throw down the lye. Laziness doesn't mix with using gloves." Xavier moved to one of the other bodies. Judging by the size of the ribcage and skull, it was a male. "Then there's this." There was a small nick in the bone just above the ankle.

"A defensive wound or offensive wound meant to disable," I recognized the nick. Someone had sliced through the Achilles' tendon. It was a great place for a petite female to attack. It was incredibly painful and made walking difficult. I knew because I had used it a few times to slow down psychopaths.

"This is the largest body. I think they cut the tendon in an offensive move. Once the tendon was completely sliced across, the victim would have been more manageable. It is also the only body to show that the blade went in and hit bone," Xavier frowned, "it's conflicting."

"You think the attacker is either young or a woman based on the bodies."

"Yes, and it makes me question the idea that it is a doctor or nurse. Our ribcage shifts slightly when we are lying down. If the other victims were standing up, the ribs are easy to see, even in the back, but lying down makes it more difficult, they hit the rib on their way into the chest cavity."

"Size could be a factor as well."

"I know," Xavier said. "I still think it's a woman."

"Female psychopaths are rare," I reminded him.

"Maybe she isn't a psychopath."

"It sucks to bury a knife up to the hilt if you feel it." I frowned at the statement. It hurt worse to be on the receiving end of said knife wound, but it left a hell of a bruise. "So, we are looking for a petite woman who had a massive bruise on her hand around the time that our victim was killed. If we factor in young and medical knowledge, we still have a huge suspect pool, because unfortunately, we have to include Austin. Young women with medical knowledge would be prolific on the University of Texas campus, not to mention the other colleges in town."

"A med student would fit," Xavier's face was grim.

"Have you eaten lately? You look pale and your face looks a little skeletal."

"I do need lunch and someone to back me up that we are looking for a female, probably petite. There's an upward angle to Nathan Jones' wound, not enough to hit bone, but enough to be noteworthy."

Xavier and I joined Fiona, Gabriel, and Lucas at a diner across from the police station. It was down-home style cooking, which in Texas seemed to mean gravy or barbecue sauce on everything. I couldn't eat barbecue sauce and I didn't eat gravy, so I ordered a grilled cheese sandwich and onion rings. Technically, I wasn't supposed to eat many fried foods either, but that was hard to do when you travelled as much as we did.

My grilled cheese had a thick slice of ham on it. I pulled it off my sandwich and scraped as much of the cheese back onto my bread as possible. They had also provided me with a cup of gravy to dip my onion rings into. I pushed it to the side. Xavier grabbed it and dumped it on his fried chicken, or whatever it was.

By the end of lunch, I had convinced Lucas we were looking for a woman. Of course, I had to use myself as an example on several occasions, but he finally agreed. Gabriel was less skeptical, but not willing to rule out that it was just a small male, and Fiona didn't care one way or the other, she just wanted us to stop talking about wound tracks at the diner. People were starting to stare at us and she didn't like the scrutiny. The rest of us were used to it. Xavier and I still smelled like the morgue. A handful of people had asked to be moved away from our table and that was before the conversation had started.

Gabriel paid for lunch using a newly issued government credit card. We had all gotten them after returning from Detroit. Malachi's team had received identical cards. I wasn't sure why they had issued them.

"Cain, you're with me," Gabriel announced as we left the diner. I climbed into the SUV. Everyone else climbed into a different SUV.

"I still smell like the morgue."

"I'm okay with that, I can't even smell it anymore."

"What's up?"

"Are you, you again?"

"Yes," I answered. "I had a moment in the morgue with the body of Nathan Jones. I found his body creepy. I didn't have problems with any of the others though."

"We all had problems with it," Gabriel answered. "It was the preservation compared to the others according to Lucas. We all got the heebie-jeebies, but I appreciate you being honest about it. Think you are capable of a little intimidation?"

"Oh yeah," I answered, realizing we were about to go meet the Jones family.

Seven

Emily Jones was a shell of a person. Whatever spirit she had once possessed was completely gone. She shuffled her feet, kept her head down, and talked in a weak voice. Her husband, Victor Jones, wasn't home, but Gabriel and I had decided to wait for him. I was doing my best to contain the violence that I wanted to unleash. I was angry at Emily Jones for not protecting her son and even angrier when her daughter, a gangly twelve year old that had the look of the lost, entered the home and immediately set about doing her homework as quietly as possible.

The daughter, Lauren Jones, was already starting to look like her mother. She avoided all eye contact with Gabriel and me. Her shoulders were hunched forward, as if expecting a blow to land on her at any moment. Her face was pale with black circles under her eyes. She wasn't broken yet, but the process was in progress.

Emily kept offering us something to drink, but refused to talk about her son without her husband present. It grated on my nerves. It made my head hurt. It set my teeth on edge. I bit back on the contemptuous things I wanted to tell her. I kept having to remind myself that she was a victim too. My anger needed to be focused on Victor Jones and not Emily. It would certainly do damage to Lauren if I went off on her mother. I'd be no better than her father. Besides, it might do both of them some good to see a small woman like me put Victor Jones in his place. Secretly, I hoped he swung at me, so I would have a reason to sate my blood lust.

Victor Jones was not an imposing man. He was short for a guy, only about 5 feet and eight inches tall. He was thin with a little muscle buried beneath sallow skin. His teeth were bad. His eyes tinged yellow. He was either a meth user or a very hard drinker, or both.

"US Marshal Gabriel Henders," Gabriel stood up as the man entered the house, I did not, afraid I would leap across the space between us and begin throttling him just for existing. "We are here because we found your son, Nathan."

"Good, I hope the little bastard is in jail." Victor did not shake Gabriel's extended hand and Gabriel dropped it after a moment. The calm descended like a fog, a welcome fog, one that I had actually missed during my time with a brain tumor. It was a familiar lack of nothingness. The anger I had been feeling earlier was gone, replaced by a dark void of humanity. Even rage wouldn't penetrate the darkness, because it was an emotion and here, I had none of those. Only the primal urge, a need too dark to have a name, remained within me.

My heartbeat slowed. My blood pressure dropped. My gaze locked onto Victor Jones, refusing to break contact with my prey. Time itself slowed, allowing me to see the world in ways that other people never would.

Victor's heartbeat picked up. It pulsed in the veins of his neck. Tiny beads of sweat, almost too small to be noticed, began to form. His pupils dilated and his mouth opened. Whatever he was going to say didn't come out. Instead, he made a strangled chirping sound and his mouth flapped like a fish's for a few moments. Then he regained some of his composure and looked away from me.

"Your son was murdered, Mr. Jones. His body was found inside a well yesterday, just outside of town. Can either of you think of anyone that would want your son dead?" Gabriel sat back down.

"No," Emily Jones started to speak, but stopped.

"No." Victor gave her a glare.

"Did you do it, Mr. Jones?" I asked. "Did you kill your son and dump him in an abandoned well, hoping no one would find him? Did you kill the others found in the well?"

"I want you to leave, now," Mr. Jones stood up.

"Sit down," I told him. "You will answer our questions here or you will answer them at the police station."

"Get out!" He shouted at me. I remained seated and turned my attention to Emily. She visibly wilted under my gaze. Her hands began to tremble.

"Do you know if your husband killed your son? Have you entertained the possibility?" I asked her. The tremble moved throughout her entire body. She had considered it. "Do you care that he was murdered?"

"Of course," she squeaked out. Victor gave her another menacing glance.

"I said to get out!" Victor shouted again, trying to prove he was bigger than I was. His anger was directed solely at me and not just because of the accusations, but because I was smaller than him and he had felt intimidated by me. For a moment, he had lost his composure, let his terrified family see him afraid and now he had to regain it. It would be a mistake. I shot a quick glance into the kitchen. Lauren sat motionless at the table, her eyes staring at her homework, hoping to go unnoticed.

"We will be back, Mr. Jones," Gabriel stood up. I followed his lead. We both walked outside and got into the SUV. Gabriel didn't start the engine, but he turned the key and rolled down the windows. He lit a cigarette and handed it to me. "How long?"

"Five minutes, maybe ten, if he looks out the window." I took a drag of the cigarette. "Drive down the block, park at the end of the street, we'll walk back, smoking our cigarettes. It should be in progress by then."

"And if she doesn't scream?" Gabriel asked.

"Lauren will. Victor will be shouting down the walls."

"It's good to have you back, the real you back."

"That's twice I've heard that today," I said as Gabriel started the SUV and pulled up the street. He hid the SUV on the wrong side of the street, behind a large truck. There seemed to be several of those. We both got out, closing our doors quietly.

As we moved down the street, we didn't talk. The only sounds were our feet against the pavement, a quiet thumping noise. Gabriel had drawn his gun. I had not. I wanted to feel the blood seep through my fingers. We stopped near a large tree. Gabriel leaned against it as he finished his cigarette. I kept my ears tuned for the sounds of distress.

The tinkling of breaking glass drifted to me. I tilted my head and tossed my cigarette. Gabriel pushed off the tree. We began moving again, getting closer to the house. In front of the neighbor's, we heard a muffled scream. I broke into a jog, Gabriel followed, not daring to step in front of me. The calm had not lifted and Victor Jones was about to meet his own personal demon, up close. Another cry, this one louder than the scream, reached me as I jumped onto the porch, skipping the steps entirely.

Victor Jones was unprepared for me to burst through his front door. It shattered and cracked as I put my full weight against it. The hinges squealed as they were pulled out of the frame. Victor had a belt raised over his head, caught in mid-strike, he didn't know whether to follow through with the motion, drop it, or change his target.

I didn't give him time to make a decision. My shoulder caught him at diaphragm level and my momentum picked him up. His feet dangled for a moment, before he slammed into the wall behind him. The sheetrock cracked and caved in where his body landed. I drew back and landed a blow squarely on his jaw before he could gather his breath. He yelped. I grabbed him by the front of his shirt, twisting it around my hands, and yanked him out of the broken wall.

Lauren Jones rushed into the room. She grabbed her mother and the two huddled together near the chair I had vacated minutes earlier. They both sobbed. I looked at their tears and felt nothing.

Victor struggled to get his footing, as I jerked him around by his shirt. He tugged against me in futile spastic motions. His hands flailed at my face and arms, trying to stop me from manhandling him. I grabbed one of those flailing arms above the wrist. It twisted in my hand and I yanked, feeling the bone snap beneath my hand. Victor cried out in pain, his flailing becoming more desperate. His hand, limp and useless, was already showing signs of swelling. The remaining good hand clawed at me, raking dirty, broken fingernails across my skin. They created welts, but didn't draw blood.

I punched him again, this time connecting with his ribs. The air exited his lungs with a great whooshing noise. His knees buckled and his back arched. I landed another body blow that forced us both to the ground. My hand untangled from his shirt, letting me stay on my knees as he curled into a fetal position. I stood up and stared at him. He was injured but not bleeding. The darkness wanted blood. Without thinking, I raised my steel-plated boot up and brought it down on his lower leg. There was a snapping noise followed by a scream. When my boot hit the floor, it left a bloody footprint. The bone stuck out of the leg. Blood and marrow oozed from it.

Gabriel touched my shoulder, cautiously. I turned and glared at him for a moment. Then the darkness lifted as Victor Jones began sobbing at my feet. He blubbered unintelligibly through snot and tears. Emily and Lauren stood up, both seemed afraid to approach. They clung to each other.

"I don't think he'll be hurting either of you again." Gabriel took them outside.

I stooped down, getting as close as possible to Victor.

"Not so big and tough now. You got your ass kicked by a girl. The front page tomorrow will read, 'US Marshal Aislinn Cain takes down abusive husband', and it'll have a photo of you, being wheeled out on a gurney, and me, standing beside the gurney, putting you in handcuffs, you son of a bitch. I know you didn't kill your son, but you created the circumstances that made him vulnerable to attack. Every time you even think about raising your voice let alone your hand, I hope you remember how much that broken leg hurts. Because next time, I'll break open your fucking skull and scoop your tiny, warped brain out with my bare hands." I stood back up, checked my clothing for blood, and made room for the paramedics.

"Wow," one said as he looked at Victor's leg.

"He resisted arrest," I answered.

"Did you kick him with lead boots?"

"No, I stomped on him with steel-plated boots."

"Sir, I'm going to roll you onto a board," the paramedic said. I'd seen it done plenty of times, but never as roughly as these two did it. When Victor cried out in pain, I would have sworn one of them gave a small smile. I guess I wasn't the only one that thought he had gotten what he deserved.

Eight

"Feel better?" Lucas asked as we sat in a police conference room.

"Are you talking about the chunk of brain they removed, or breaking Victor Jones's leg?"

"Both."

"Yes, much," I answered. "However, my favorite part of this neurological roller coaster has been the return of my ability to break someone's leg and enjoy it."

"He deserved it," a detective said as he entered the room. "Police are called out there every couple of months because of the beating he has thrown someone in the house. We are always told they fell down the stairs or something ridiculous like that. I don't believe anyone is going to feel sorry for him. If you'd broken both his legs, we might have thrown a parade in your honor."

"Must not be a lot of abusive men in San Marcos," Lucas stated.

"Oh, we have a few, but none like Victor Jones. You'd never know it now, but Emily was homecoming queen and very popular when she was in school. Then she went to college, fell for Victor, and the rest has been a train wreck. Victor made her drop out of college, and then they moved in with her parents because she got pregnant. We suspect Victor killed her parents for the life insurance, but we could never prove it."

"How'd they die?" I asked.

"Car accident, on their way here to report him for abusing their daughter. His sister has been trying to get charges filed, but Emily always told a different story. We've always figured it was because he had threatened to kill her, too. Now, she can get away from him. He'll be going to prison for a long time, possibly for the rest of his miserable life." The detective sat down. "We haven't been introduced, I'm Ben Hight, I was the detective called out to find the bodies, and you need no introduction, Marshal

Cain, and that was before you got hold of Victor Jones."

"How'd you guys find the bodies? The report says the well was abandoned," I asked.

"It was. The Hawthornes decided to have it filled in because their dog wouldn't stop barking at it. However, before it could be filled in, they had to make sure it hadn't become contaminated and that's when the inspector found the bodies," Detective Hight told me.

"How long had the dog been barking at it?"

"Off and on for the last year, but non-stop for the last month, according to the owners."

"So, he'd bark as the bodies decomposed, then stop, then start when a new one went in," I told Lucas. Lucas just nodded. "About a year, off and on, so the first body went into the well about this time last year and the newest one went in a month ago."

"Don't suppose you can get a list of all abandoned properties, wells, barns, sheds, etc. in the area?" Lucas asked.

"I can ask people to report it, but we don't keep those kinds of records, why?"

"None of our bodies had hesitation marks on them," I told him. "A serial killer doesn't just start out and have perfect kills. The first one or two or five, usually show some signs of hesitation, because they want to do it again, but they aren't as committed to doing it as they are after they've been at it a while without getting caught. Also, the killer got lazy during the disposal of a body, and that's something that is gained through experience and confidence."

"In other words, there are more bodies, somewhere," Lucas told him.

"I'll get some maps and show you everything I know of," Detective Hight left the room.

"Five a year, for an unknown number of years, that could get pretty high," Fiona commented from the corner of the room. She was currently running Xavier's dental x-rays against all the x-rays in the missing persons' database.

"I think we found five, because five was all they could put in the well. It wasn't very wide, getting bodies down it was not ideal. However, it is close to a small road, one that rarely gets used. You pull up, and it's maybe five steps, drop the body in, and pull away, all without being seen because there's a big shed blocking the view of the well from the house and no neighbors." I remembered the pictures Xavier had sent me. "My full thoughts are that the killer has been at it longer than a year and has been rotating disposal sites."

Detective Hight returned with maps of the area. He unrolled them on the table and pulled a red marker from his pocket. He circled a small area.

"This is the Hawthorne place. The only thing on their property was the well." He began to circle other areas. Sometimes empty fields, sometimes arrow-like symbols, and occasionally he scribbled a note next to it. We watched him mark twenty-three different spots.

"Great, good thing I brought my boots," I said looking at the maps. "We'll have to search all of them and we should have Gabriel do something to find other areas."

"You really want to search all these areas?" Detective Hight asked.

"Yes. Do you have access to any cadaver dogs?" I asked.

"I'll call the Rangers," Detective Hight left.

"Yeah, they're busy searching for UFOs that abduct young women," I said to the door as it closed.

"What?" Lucas asked.

"Nothing," I shook my head. "If I'm right about the rotating sites, we probably won't need the dogs."

"Think you can out-sniff a bloodhound?" Lucas smiled.

"No, I can't smell cancerous growths under the skin, but I do pretty well at finding decaying flesh."

"Dogs will be here tomorrow," Detective Hight returned.

"Good," I answered, looking at the maps. "We still have daylight left, so we'll check some of these today. The bodies aren't being buried, just shoved in things, which will work to our advantage."

"Follow her nose," Lucas stood up and shrugged. "Where's the smallest place? We'll start there."

"Abandoned shack on the outskirts of town." The detective looked at Lucas reluctantly.

"Ace has a super sniffer. She can smell decaying feet shoved in socks and half frozen, hanging from an electrical line." Lucas smiled. I frowned at him.

"She damn near killed me for burning sage," Fiona added. "In her defense, I didn't realize how sensitive she was to smells, or that she could smell the residue for days afterwards." I turned and frowned at her.

"Frowning won't help," Lucas told me. "Neither will Tasering us."

I walked out instead. Lucas and Hight followed, as I knew they would. Detective Hight jumped into a car, the first I had ridden in since arriving in Texas, and started the engine. I shoved Lucas, with his long legs, into the backseat.

We drove in silence. There was less traffic and less scenery as we exited San Marcos onto a two-lane blacktop road. The grass was a vibrant green, lush and full looking. Trees were covered with leaves. Heat shimmered off the asphalt. We crossed a river that looked like a very big creek and were instantly surrounded by pasture and cropland again. The farms were plentiful, but modest. The spring rains had been good to the ground and early planted crops. Hight turned off the highway and onto a gravel road.

Dust kicked up behind us. The rains had been less kind to the gravel; parts of it had washed out. The car bucked and jerked over the washboard like dirt. Hight lowered our speed, before turning into a driveway.

Calling the place a shack was generous. It was a single room building, a little bit larger than a shed, with an outhouse. The wood was dark from years of weathering without paint. The small porch creaked with the gentle breeze that blew. It lacked windows or even frames for windows. The doorknob was rusted and flaky.

A large crow squawked from a nearby fence post. We all turned to look at it. Its black feathers looked glossy in the sunlight. If I had been superstitious, I would have considered the crow a bad omen. I should have been superstitious.

Detective Hight pulled against the door, not the knob. It gave an audible pop. The air rushed out to surround us in its pungent aroma. Lucas and Hight fought the urge to gag. I rubbed peppermint balm under my nose. It tingled, but kept the smell from invading my nostrils and sticking in my throat. I passed it around.

The body inside was bloated. The eyes stared at the doorway, as if it were expecting company. Blood had covered the shirt and the wall above the body's head. The gun lay between the legs.

"Not ours," I said, turning away.

"Probably a suicide," Lucas said, "but Xavier should look at him anyway."

"It's Greg Collins," Detective Hight said. "He lost his job about a month ago, went out drinking with friends and never came home."

"How old?" I asked.

"Thirty-nine, has a wife and two kids."

"Not our killer then, he's too old." I watched the crow. It returned my watchful gaze. The breeze ruffled its feathers and the bird appeared to shiver before taking flight. My eyes followed it until it had disappeared. Some legends consider the crow an evil bird. Some considered it a messenger of doom. Others believed it was one of the few animals that could cross between the spirit realm and the world of the living, and so ferried lost souls to the other side.

For the briefest moment, my mind wondered if his soul had been trapped in the shack, watching his body rot, while the crow waited to take his soul to whatever awaited us after life. It was hard to believe in things I couldn't see. It was just as hard not to get wrapped up in wanting to believe. Facts could prove or disprove just about any argument, and there were always two sides. Knowing both without forming an opinion was a slippery slope. It was just as easy to believe aliens were mutilating cattle for food as it was not to believe, once you understood both arguments.

The lowing of a cow, very close by, shook me from my reverie. The beast had lumbered within a hundred feet of the shack, held in by the pitiful fence where the crow had sat. I giggled.

"What's funny?" Lucas asked.

"I was just thinking it was a good thing aliens liked to eat cows. It would be really difficult to track down serial killing aliens."

"Occasionally, I worry about your train of thought." Lucas started walking towards the car. I snickered one more time at the cow, and then joined him.

Nine

Being alone in a dark room, in a strange place, can be unsettling. I was fine with that. It was the dark, strange room, and not being alone that bothered me. My gun was trained on the silhouette of a man as he moved towards a lamp.

"You were talking in your sleep, loudly," Xavier said as the light came on.

"So you thought you'd sneak about in my room? That doesn't sound like a very intelligent thing to do."

"I didn't think about it before I did it," Xavier agreed. "I did bring Lucas, just in case."

"Did I say anything interesting?"

"I'm fairly sure you were arguing with God over serial killing aliens and adopted puppies."

"Too much time spent with Malachi and my mother," I sighed and lowered the gun. "I agreed to read a list of recommended books he put together. Some he obviously put on the list to irritate me. Others were meant to persuade me to the dark side of animal mutilations and aliens. I agreed to let my mother move in and she adopted us a puppy. Obviously, I was easy to manipulate during the first couple of days after brain removal."

"We didn't remove any of your brain. We removed a mass of damaged cells that had rapidly grown due to repetitive brain injury. You did get really good drugs afterwards though. You're the one that suggested your mother move in with you. I think it was because Malachi was still insinuating the two of you move in together," Xavier said.

"I should Taser him just on principle."

"Yep," Xavier agreed. "Do you want us to leave you alone to go back to arguing with God?"

"That would be nice."

"I want to check your head first."

"It has been almost two months. My head is fine."

"You're talking in your sleep."

"I've always talked in my sleep. Want to try another reason?"

"No," Xavier walked over to me and moved my hair around. "We'll go with, you have to have my approval to stay working, so you'll let me look at it all I want. I just want to make sure your scalp is growing back and that you haven't developed a soft spot."

"Fine," I sighed, as he gently moved around the area where they had removed my skull and sewn my skin back over it. "Well?" I asked as he finished.

"It's healing well," he answered. "The bone seems to be hardening just fine."

He'd already checked my reflexes and thinking ability. For the first month, he'd required weekly blood tests to check the levels of epinephrine, norepinephrine, and dopamine. All had returned to normal. Aside from Xavier's nagging, I thought I was as healthy as ever.

"Good, go away, so I can go back to sleep." I adjusted my pajama pants; glow in the dark moons with mice chewing on them. My mom had given them to me for Easter and yes, at twenty-eight, I still got an Easter basket. That said, the candy had been eaten mostly by her, I had mainly wanted the pajamas.

They both said goodnight and left. I laid back down, but couldn't fall back asleep. Then my mind latched onto the idea of another female psychopath. One skilled enough not to hit ribs while stabbing her victim, but strong enough to bury the knife not just to the hilt, but also with the force needed to leave the button mark. Yet, she hadn't been able to carry some of her victims farther than a few feet. To me, it meant the weight wasn't the issue. It had to be the awkwardness of the dead weight. It would be like carrying an oversized box or trying to drag a half-stuffed mattress.

I was considered average in build and height. At five feet, three inches tall, I weighed 132 pounds, but could lift significantly more than my own body weight. However, moving Lucas or Malachi would be awkward because of the sheer size difference. I might be able to throw Malachi over my shoulder, but his feet or head would drag the ground. There was no way I could toss Lucas over my shoulder. Dragging either of them would be easier, but only if they were totally unconscious. They would have the center of balance to fight me if they were awake, taking my feet out from under me.

The male skeleton we'd found was approximately six feet. With skin, muscle, and organs Xavier estimated he was two hundred pounds. Dead, I'd be able to drag him at least a hundred yards. Even living with the injury to the tendon, I could have dragged him about that.

This meant that either our female didn't have ASPD, or she was smaller than I was in both height and weight. Given the lack of violence in the kills, it didn't feel like she was being fueled by rage or hate. My mouth kept saying mercy kills, but that didn't feel right either. Mercy kills were merciful and meant to preserve dignity. Nathan Jones was in a bad situation. The others might have been too, but the bodies were just dumped. There was no mercy or dignity in that.

Of course, every kill has an element of narcissism. Killing was as close to playing God as a person could get. However, narcissism still didn't explain the way she chose to kill. It was as if we were missing a piece of the puzzle, a big piece, and that was throwing everything off. Her skills and knowledge said experience, but the victims seemed impulsive, victims of chance and circumstance. Males were more interested in victims of opportunity than females.

There were also exceptions to every rule. Maybe we did have a female psychopath preying on high risk teenagers. She could be a med student at the University of Texas, but why would she hunt here? Or dispose of the bodies here? Was she a local commuting between San Marcos and Austin?

It seemed disposing of bodies in Austin would be more logical. San Antonio was just south of here. It was a straight shot from Austin to San Antonio on a major interstate. Disposing of bodies in San Marcos didn't make sense.

I called Xavier's cell phone and could hear it ringing on the other side of the wall. It rang twice before he answered. His voice said he was annoyed.

"Did you figure out anything useful with the bodies today?" I asked, ignoring his irritation.

"The youngest was a fourteen year old female, and the oldest was a seventeen year old male. However, judging by the order they were in the hole, the fourteen year old went in first, followed by another female of the same approximate age, then the seventeen year old male, then Nathan Jones, and then an unidentified female that I'm guessing is younger than the two males. Why?"

"Just wondering." I hung up.

A terrible thought was forming. The age disparity wasn't huge, but it was interesting. Young teen girls looked up to older teen girls. Teen boys liked teen girls roughly their age, give or take a year. Seventeen-year-old boys weren't likely to sneak off with fourteen-year-old girls. They were likely to sneak off with eighteen-year-old girls and sixteen-year-old girls. A short teen male would be a target for bullies, but a petite teen girl would be popular.

Thinking it was terrifying, but saying it out loud would be worse. My niece was a cute, petite, teen girl, and from what I had been told, she was popular. It was hard to imagine her killing a classmate, but she had the genes to do it. Cassie wouldn't know how to insert a knife between ribs and damage the heart, though. That was more adult than she could muster.

My mind was pretty sure that Cassie wasn't sixteen or seventeen and I knew she wasn't eighteen.

Was she a good basis for comparison as a result? I didn't know. The clock said it was about three in the morning. I called Elle anyway.

"How old is Cassie?" I asked as she answered her phone, instantly awake. In our family, three a.m. phone calls were a bad thing.

"What?" She asked.

"How old is Cassie? I can't remember."

"This is not important enough for a wee hours of the morning call."

"It might be," I said.

"No, Aislinn, it isn't. She turned sixteen her last birthday. You will be twenty-nine on your birthday. Anything else?"

"Nope, that's what I needed to know."

"Do I want to ask why?"

"It's a case, we found three teen girls, and it was bothering me because of Cassie and her age. Is she popular? Does she do sports? Is she in any clubs?"

"Yes, she plays soccer and cheerleading. She's on the student council and the yearbook."

"Ok, thanks, go back to bed." I hung up.

That answered that. My niece was sixteen and popular. She played sports and participated in school activities. She and I were very different. I'd been a nerd, not a joiner or participator. Malachi had been popular. This left me conflicted. Her popularity should have made her low risk for being like me, but Malachi was proof that this was not the case. He was popular because he was damaged and hid it well. Without having to deal with real emotions, he could fake whatever was correct for the situation, and it made him popular.

Tearing myself away from thoughts of Cassie, which were getting me nowhere and making me feel as if I needed to have Xavier give her a personality test; I tried to go back to the case. A teen girl would explain everything except the experience.

I could have done it at sixteen. I could have slipped a knife between the correct ribs to puncture the heart or lungs. I could have done it at twelve. I might have even had the steady hands and forethought to put on gloves, cover my hair, and keep from contaminating the crime scene with hair and other person specific forensics. I might have even been able to have the foresight to cover my tracks with lye and other caustic materials.

Oh yeah, at sixteen I could have been a serial killer, but could I tell that to Gabriel? I wasn't as convinced about that.

The Party

Monday held two finals for Jess. Her history final was worth one-fifth of her grade. That meant failing it would drop her to a B in the class. Jess had never had a B, but history wasn't her best subject. The other was English, and included a five-page paper that was to be done beforehand, and to give examples of literature themes from a specific book they had read during the year. She was about half done with the paper and was running out of things to write about.

She knew there had been several themes and motifs within *Ethan Frome*, but she had only thought of one of each. As such, she had discussed the oppression of winter and the symbolism behind red for nearly a page each. Her notes didn't seem to make sense anymore. They mentioned sledding, society v. desire, illnesses as a reflection of turmoil, and suicide. She wasn't sure which were themes and which were motifs. Getting it wrong would damage her grade. Her desire to reread *Ethan Frome* was zero.

None of it mattered, not tonight. Tonight there was Simon. Simon Westbrook was *the guy* in Jess's mind. He was smart, attractive, and active in the community. He would be the perfect addition to her life and a trophy on her arm for senior year.

In her fantasies, Simon and Jess walked the halls of school holding hands. Their fellow classmates would gape at them in awe and envy. They'd arrive together in the morning and leave together in the afternoon. He'd carry her books. She'd wear his letterman's jacket. After high school, they'd both go away to college and maintain a long distance relationship. Pictures of them together would plaster their dorm room walls.

They'd end up at the same place for grad school. Both would work part time to pay the bills for the apartment they would share. Simon would get a degree in something respectable; engineering or law. She'd follow in her mother's footsteps and go to

Med School to become a doctor. Not a pediatrician, but an ER doctor or something. Maybe Simon would prove an aptitude for medicine and become a doctor too.

Then they'd come back here or maybe Austin or San Antonio. They'd get jobs in their respected fields. They'd have perfect lives as they built their family and their dream home. They'd both volunteer in the community. Their kids would be active in sports and hold high grades. They'd once again be looked upon with awe and envy.

The problem was getting Simon to realize it. Her advances had always been rebuffed in the past. For some unfathomable reason, he didn't seem to want her. Jess had searched for all possible answers for his lack of interest and always came to the same conclusion, he was playing hard to get. There was no logical reason for him not to want her. She was attractive, smart, athletic, and active in the community. She had few, if any, faults. Younger girls looked up to her. Girls her own age wanted to be her. Even older girls wanted to be her.

Shawn Steiger tapped her shoulder, breaking her from her reverie. It irritated her, but she tried not to show it. Shawn was holding two Solo cups filled with a red fluid, lighter in color than the cups that held them.

"Want a drink?" He offered her one of the glasses.

"Thanks." She took it and managed a sip of the red fluid. The taste of vodka was strong under the fruit punch. As the alcohol passed into her stomach, it flopped and gurgled, making her feel queasy. She managed a smile. Shawn was a good guy, not her type, but a good guy nonetheless. There was no reason to be rude to him. Besides, he was good friends with Simon. If she worked it right, she might be able to figure out what Simon's problem was.

"I haven't seen Becky. Is she here?" Shawn asked. Jess turned to look at the guy. He wasn't real tall and he was a bit of a dork. Becky would be grossed out knowing Shawn had the hots for her.

"Yeah, she's around. I think she was going to find Matt, but I don't know where she disappeared to." Jess gave a quick glance at Simon. He still hadn't acknowledged that she existed. He was drinking with a few guys, laughing and talking. She liked his laugh. She liked the way his lips moved when he talked. "So, what's the deal with Simon?"

"Simon?" Shawn looked at her for a moment. "Oh, you mean why hasn't he agreed to go on a date with you?"

"Essentially," Jess said.

"He thinks you're too absorbed by your books to be much fun, and you kinda are. I mean you have fun, but not a lot of it. I was really surprised when you said you were coming tonight, what with finals and all next week. I figured you'd be busy studying."

"Oh," Jess frowned, "did you tell Simon any of this?"

"Sort of," Shawn blushed. "He asked, and since I have known you for more than a decade, I answered. What do you want Simon for anyway? He keeps a whole lot of girls on the side. He's never been faithful to a girlfriend. All he ever talks about is who he's having sex with this week."

"Maybe he just hasn't found the right girl."

"Ha, yeah, right, Simon will never find the right girl. He'll grow up, get married, and have mistresses that drive his poor wife nuts. He's like that. You could do better. Any girl could," Shawn answered.

"Hey, let's go for a ride," Jess suggested. "I found a great little spot recently where the light pollution isn't as bad. Just for old times. Remember how we used to climb up on the roof of your house and look at the stars with your telescope?"

"Well, since Becky is still hung up on Matt, sure, why not, but no talking about Simon. You shouldn't debase yourself that way. You're better than him."

They left together, in the middle of someone doing a keg stand. Jess was pretty sure it was Matt doing it, since Becky was in the crowd, paying her no attention. That was fine with Jess, the fewer people that noticed them leave, the better.

The darkened spring night was lovely. There wasn't a cloud in the sky. They drove with the windows down. The moon was full and hung low in the sky, helping to illuminate the road they were on.

Poor Shawn, Jess thought. He was always going to be the other guy. The guy that was friends with guys, but also the butt of their jokes. The guy who was too sensitive to be really masculine. The guy every girl liked to be friends with, but didn't want to date. He'd lust after girls like Becky all his life and never obtain one. They'd lived across the street from one another since she was four years old. Honestly, she was doing him a favor. She was saving him from the harsh realities of the world.

They arrived at an old ranger's station. It had been abandoned when they built a new one a half dozen years ago. It was too far from the beaten path to be helpful to most people, hence its replacement. If she strained her eyes, she could just make out the lights from the replacement station through the woods.

"Turn around, I have a surprise for you and I need to get ready," Jess said. Shawn smiled and did as she asked. He'd always trusted her. Jess undressed to her bra and panties. She put her clothes as far away from them as possible and covered them with a discarded magazine.

She did take the knife out of her jeans pocket. She walked over to Shawn, placed one arm over his shoulder and whispered for him to turn around.

He did. His eyes widened as he took in the fact that she was nearly nude in the moonlight. She leaned against him. She tousled his hair, feeling him become erect against her. He leaned in to kiss her and she plunged the blade into his throat. Warm blood spilled over her hand. It fell against the floor like heavy raindrops during a storm.

The surprise on his face was replaced by anger and fear. His brain had yet to realize he was going to die. His wound was too great for any other outcome. A choking, strangled noise slipped from his lips, the last bit of air escaping from his throat. Jess knew the blade had cut into his windpipe. The wound sucked at the metal with a wet sound. Jess waited.

Shawn fell forward, his body spasming one final time. She reached down and rolled him over. His arms flopped because of the movement. His eyes stared at the ceiling, not seeing the spider webs and other insects taking residence in the abandoned station.

Jess pulled the knife out. She had to twist and jerk at the same time. It should have hurt her hand, but she didn't feel the pain. She cleaned up with water from the trunk of her car. She kept gallon jugs of it in there for emergencies. Never knew when you would get stranded on a hot day in the middle of nowhere.

After cleaning herself, she took another container out of the trunk. This one was a white plastic jug. It was heavy, even to her. There was a skull and crossbones on the label along with the bare essentials in text. The skull and crossbones were because it contained high amounts of sulfuric acid. It was amazing how many corrosive chemicals were in drain cleaner and it was available over the counter.

Ten

It would be safe to say that the men in my life are very chatty. Their constant use of small talk was astounding. This morning was no different. Two of them were swapping nonsense about something that I didn't understand, because I did not have the gift of making small talk.

We were waiting for Fiona and Xavier. They were still doing something with computers, facial structures and missing persons' files, but promised to join us soon. I was thinking about the Capitol Hill Thug who stalked Denver, Colorado from 1900-1901. He did manage to kill a few women, but mostly, he just seemed to enjoy stalking them and bashing them over the head with a pipe. Death was therefore unintentional, but occasionally, inevitable. Any time you bash someone on the head with a pipe, death could be a side effect.

The Thug had highlighted the ineptitude of the Denver Police Department. The case had intruded upon me as I dressed this morning to come into the San Marcos Police Department. Not because the police were inept, but because of the lack of rage.

Lucas would argue that hitting someone on the head with a metal or wooden object was an act of rage. I would disagree. A single blow is not an act of rage, but an act of sadism. The Thug could have continued bashing in the skulls of his female victims until their brains spilled out upon the ground. He didn't. However, a single blow to the head was also not merciful, which was why my brain latched onto it.

There were similarities between a man giving a good blow to a woman and then fleeing, and our killer with her single stab wound to the heart. Both acts lacked rage, neither was merciful. That kind of kill still required a person to get up close and personal. There was pleasure in the act, not the side effects. The Thug killed three women, but attacked about ten. Our killer had definitely killed five people, but that was because they were the only ones we had found.

Concentrating on motiveless unsolved historical crimes was better than focusing on the small talk around me. I was sure The Thug had a motive for his crimes, but it was never revealed. He didn't rob or rape his victims. Aggression wasn't part of the attack. The wound, while lethal, wasn't aggressive. She wasn't repeatedly stabbing her victims after they died. She wasn't plunging the knife into their eyeballs or cutting off their noses. Those would have been extremely aggressive actions.

It ruled out rage, hatred, anger, jealousy, envy, and obsession. Those emotions fueled aggression. The kills were emotionless. This did ease my mind ever so slightly. Teens were filled with conflicting, hormone driven emotions that flood every part of their lives. That's why high school is like a badly written soap opera. The chances of my niece sneaking up on her classmates and stabbing them through the heart before slipping away into the gathering crowd were slim to none. She was more likely to go bat shit crazy and stab them so many times, light would be able to shine through the many holes.

Mentally, I realized that my niece was not physically in San Marcos stabbing her unknown classmates. I was still having a small problem with transference. I didn't think it was because of the tumor. Some part of me had grown and I was acutely aware of it. Having friends, family, and some understanding of myself had allowed me to realize I did not and could not exist in a vacuum. No matter how much I enjoyed quiet and solitude, I needed people to keep me human and no one was better qualified than those that accepted both parts of me. Unfortunately, this meant they were indispensable in my life, and I now walked the line that Patterson had once walked.

I pushed aside thoughts of Patterson, Cassie, my mother, and the expensive hybrid puppy that I now co-owned. Xavier and Fiona had finally arrived. So had our cadaver dogs and their handlers.

"We've identified all the victims and they were all locals," Xavier told us. "If Aislinn is right and this group of bodies isn't our killer's first, then it seems logical that other victims will also be local."

"Our serial is a local," Detective Hight sighed. "That's the last thing this town needs."

"No offense, but that's the last thing any town needs. Even large cities do not need serial killers preying on teenagers. If all serial killers did it, we'd lose entire generations and there would be a serious population decline," I said absentmindedly.

"That was depressing," Fiona said.

"But true," I shrugged. "Serial killers already impact population growth, but it is spread out among all genders and ages, which minimalizes the damage. If they didn't, we'd have a bottleneck much like the Soviet Union did during and immediately following World War II."

"I'm sure that's a fascinating story, but we have a serial killer to catch," Gabriel reminded me.

"So did they," I quipped. "Although, Stalin may have been more mass murderer than serial killer. I'm sure the Soviets had their fair share of serials during those turbulent and trying years of Stalinism. He definitely did not deserve statues built in his honor."

Lucas looked at me. I stopped talking. However, that didn't stop my brain from running. It was attempting to calculate what the modern population of Russia would be if Stalin and World War II hadn't happened. It was a considerable amount, nearly rivaling China. Communism might have survived if the population had been there to support it.

"Now that the history lesson is done," Gabriel glared at me, "we've divided up the area in a grid. We have four cadaver dogs at our disposal. We'll split up, each of us going out with a dog and small squad. If we find anything, we'll call in Reece to come look at the bodies. Any questions?"

"If Reece is on call, that makes three of us," I pointed out.

"Marshal Stewart will be accompanying a dog," Gabriel told me. I raised an eyebrow and Fiona looked a little green around the gills. She didn't do fieldwork.

"Great, who wants to go traipsing the county with the nutter?" I asked the group of policemen that were gathering. There were some confused looks.

"Marshal Cain means herself. She isn't really..." Gabriel stopped. He was going to say that I wasn't really crazy, but this would have been a lie.

"Cain attracts violent people, just something to be aware of when you go with her."

I held out my hands and shrugged. It was true. Violent people were attracted to me like butterflies to a corpse.

"I'll join her group," a stout man with a dog answered. I smiled at him, the fake kind. The real one would send him running for cover and might have scared the dog too. It took about twenty minutes to get organized. While most officers were being assigned, my group was voluntary. It spoke volumes.

Another twenty minutes and we were on the road. Our destination was an old farm. The family had built a new house on the land, more than a hundred acres away from the other. As a result, the old house had been left abandoned.

It showed. The windows were gone. The paint was gone. The roof had collapsed in one section. Rot had set in. Termites were doing the rest of the work. It didn't look or sound stable as we wandered up to it.

I had four volunteers. Two men, two women, I was impressed. Someone was giving background on the house and family. I tuned them out, listening instead to the house. It creaked and groaned despite there being no breeze. Its own weight was its worst enemy.

Ranger Young was having the same thoughts I was having. We both exchanged glances before turning our attention back to the house. I wasn't sure how much his Doberman weighed, but I was worried about it getting trapped in the house.

Dobermans were air-scenting dogs. They got the smell of decomp in the air and would follow it. I had never worked with a Doberman, but I had seen other breeds used. The stereotype was either German Shepherds or bloodhounds, but the two were very different types of dogs. Shepherds, like Dobermans, are air-scenters, while bloodhounds searched by sniffing the ground and are primarily used to track a single individual. I had worked with some spaniels in the past, as well as German Shepherds, because normally, we needed cadaver dogs and ground sniffing just didn't help all that much.

Ranger Young unleashed his Doberman, named Nails. The dog, who had sat patiently at his trainer's side, stood up and stuck his nose in the air.

He knew it was time to go to work. We watched the dog, waiting to see where he would lead us.

Nails didn't go up the stairs to the house, as we had expected. Instead, he headed towards a barn. The barn was in better shape than the house. We followed at a fast jog. Nails picked up his pace, following his nose. He skirted around the barn and stopped, his nose still working the air, pulling all the scents out of it that he could.

He took off again, this time he wasn't trotting. He was running and keeping up with his powerful body was impossible. Young and I were able to sprint the longest, but even we had to give up and slow our pace. Young gasped, gulping in air. I watched the dog's dark coat get farther away.

His bark was sharp. It cut through the silence, making a few team members jump. I didn't startle easy. We followed his voice, a series of quick, loud barks to a shed. I didn't have to enter it. Even I could smell the decomp now.

"Good dog," I said.

"It could be a rabbit," Young told me. "Sometimes, Nails gets confused with decomp. He's mostly a search and rescue dog."

"I don't think he's confused," I said, standing about forty feet away. I brought out the jar of peppermint balm. "You can't smell it?"

"No," Young said.

"You will," I offered the balm. He stared at it. I shrugged and put it away. It was going to be bad.

Eleven

As we stood outside the door of the shed, everyone could smell it. They were holding their hands over their nose and mouth. I once again offered the balm. Everyone took it this time. Peppermint was a wonderful thing. It tingled, which was nifty, and it killed a lot of noxious odors, but left the olfactory system fast once it was washed away.

Nails lay on the ground as I opened the door. I wanted to put some of the balm on his poor nose. I couldn't imagine how bad it smelled to him. However, I knew better. I opened the door instead.

Flies, their meal suddenly interrupted, took flight. They swarmed the stale air, creating a buzzing black cloud. A few butterflies were mixed in, their brightly colored wings contrasting with the black swarm as they fluttered. They only stayed in the air a second or two, before returning to the three bodies. Butterflies were less disturbed by living people than flies.

"Don't," I put my arm up to stop Young from entering the shed. I pointed at the floor.

It was coated in a semi-tacky goo of indescribable color. It looked black, brown, red, or orange, depending on how the light hit it and how you held your head. The shed was well built. The goo showed no footprints from scavenging animals.

Most humans forgot that they were made up primarily of water. Decomposition released the water and other fluids. As the solid parts broke down, they mixed with the water and other fluids, creating these semi-tacky puddles of human goo. However, it was a slow process and most bodies were not as well protected as these, making the goo puddles rare.

Young radioed the find in. My phone instantly rang. Xavier was on the other end.

"Well protected, insect damage severe, put in here at different times," I replied curtly. "Three bodies, all look to be young, or they were midgets."

"They prefer the term 'little people'," Xavier corrected.

"Gender unavailable at this time," I snipped. "It's bad, bring floor scrapers."

"Hm, human goo."

"Lots of it." I hung up and closed the door again. No need to let the insects out. There was also no need to go traipsing in. We'd wreck the disposal site and they were all very dead.

I lit a cigarette and walked towards a tree. Nails surprisingly followed me. Young followed Nails.

"He likes you," Young said.

"What's with the name?" I asked.

"His toenails grow at an alarming rate. I've seen a lot of dead bodies, but nothing like that."

"Human decomp without scavengers in the heat. The fluids drain creating a breeding ground for bacteria. The bacteria break down the matter. It creates goo. Most bodies are found before this stage or after. Those that aren't, well, they usually are not stored in such perfect conditions as to keep the goo from draining. It's rare to find a floor or something covered in it, but it happens."

"You're one of those very smart types that knows a little bit about a lot of different stuff, aren't you?"

"No, I know a lot of stuff about a lot of stuff and I am constantly expanding my knowledge."

"I'm not sure whether to congratulate you or give you my condolences," Young said. "I had an uncle like you. Brilliant man, couldn't forget anything he learned or saw. He was a cop too. A homicide detective to be exact. He was working a case in the fifties, a serial killer on I-5. Found a dozen little girls' bodies. They caught the guy, but he was deemed not fit to stand trial. While being held at an asylum, he escaped and managed to kill two more little girls. My uncle killed him and then killed himself."

I had nothing to say to that or to Ranger Young. Nails was fine, panting near my feet, not talking to me, but Young seemed to want to fill the void. There were a few stories that came to mind. Recently, I had put a gun to my head, the result of a tumor and a migraine. It had even created feelings and I hadn't liked it. However, that was not the type of story one told others. I could share my tragic family history; grandfather a serial killer, father a cop gunned down in the line of duty, brother a mass murderer getting revenge not just for our family, but for dozens of unknown families while destroying just as many lives. Again, that was not the type of story one told others. Instead, I offered him a cigarette from my pack. He politely declined. We stood in silence as I smoked.

"You're not much of a talker," he finally said.

"If you would like a lecture on unsolved crimes or the fall of the Soviet Union or the use of torture in medieval times, I'm your girl. However, I do not chit chat about the weather or my private life."

"A genius who doesn't talk, that's new," Ranger Young said. "Are you married?"

I frowned. I was fairly certain he wasn't deaf and that I had just said I did not chit chat about my private life. Now, he was wanting to talk about marriage.

"I am a female sociopath who hunts serial killers for a living with an IQ over 160. I'm not exactly the type of girl you bring home to your mother or take on a double date with your married friends. It would be far more likely that my number would be kept in your cell phone because you belonged to a bar trivia team and needed a ringer one or two nights because your team was in second place."

"That's depressing," Young responded.

"Depression requires a deep well of emotions to pull from. I am incapable of having many deep emotions and none of them are sad." I stubbed out my cigarette.

"A sociopath hunting sociopaths. That's a novel idea."

"Not really. History would provide a very strong basis for the theory that most law enforcement before the 1900s was indeed made up of sociopaths. It would also support the idea that executioners and the ilk were most likely psychopaths. Two sides of the same coin, both working towards the enforcement of some sort of archaic law and order. Of course, it would also support that a large number of 'madness' ascribed to many criminals was in fact the exact same mental condition. The same applies to modern day, with some exceptions. Most psychopaths can fake their way through a personality exam, fewer sociopaths make it, but that is just a matter of controlling emotions. Psychopaths have fewer emotions, so it is easier to fake being well adjusted."

"Using that logic, sociopaths would be the more unstable of the two."

"Quite the opposite. While we lack empathy, sympathy, and compassion, we are capable of feeling something. Psychopaths generally have no emotions. Our killer is most likely of the psychopathic variety. The death of the victims serves some inner need to control or destroy. Lucas is more up on the babble than I am, but the difference can be illustrated as such: if I were to kill, there would be a reason, aside from just a desire to do so. A psychopath doesn't need any reason at all." I looked at the shed door, which remained closed due to the stench. "Of course, a psychopath blends in better than a sociopath in every day society. Which makes our killer more mundane appearing than is useful. Rounding up all the oddballs in town won't help us catch the killer. We'd be better off to bring in all the 'normal' people for questioning."

A car pulled up. This was unusual, as the government seemed to have an endless supply of black SUVs with tinted windows at our disposal. The irony of driving around in the sport utility version of a hearse was not lost on me. It wasn't just that they were all SUVs, usually Suburbans, but that they were always black. Not once had we hopped into a red or white one.

Xavier climbed from the driver's side of the car. I wondered how many fences and signs were showing damage within the town of San Marcos.

He nodded to me and walked over to the shed. He didn't bother with balm of any sort. As our coroner, he was immune to the smells associated with the dead. However, even he grimaced as he opened the door. Standing under the tree hadn't moved me far enough away to keep me from being able to smell it, but with the door open, it was a chore not to make a face.

A couple of other people now stepped out of the car. They looked pale and I was betting it wasn't the heat or the smell. Facing serial killers was less harrowing than riding with Xavier. Hell, being chased by crocodiles was less harrowing than riding with Xavier. They each held a bag and began the process of unpacking them.

As we watched, they transformed from human beings to white-suited androgynous non-beings. They had almost no forms, because the suits were very loose except around the hands, ankles, and face. To this, they added gloves, booties, respirators, and goggles. Xavier just slipped on booties, obviously less concerned with getting that smell or any diseases on him.

Sometimes, I couldn't decide whether he was being cavalier or everyone else was just overly cautious. I was leaning towards the first one as he entered the shed. The two suited beings joined him and they began poking and prodding at the bodies.

The flies moved as a giant unit. They buzzed loudly, their wings beating angrily in the warm air. The butterflies lazily drifted through the door. One attempted to alight on the arm of one of the officers that had come with me. The officer beat at it crazily. I tried not to smile at his concern. Most people never understood that while butterflies and moths liked the sweet nectar of flowers, they also liked the salty goo of decomposition. Every butterfly or moth ever to touch a living person had also made a meal of something dead. The officer would probably never look at a butterfly the same way.

One landed on my arm, a large Monarch with exceptionally bright markings. Unlike the officer, I didn't bat at the insect or attempt to keep it from landing on me. Its tiny tongue poked at my skin, licking off the salt that collected on the flesh. It tickled.

"Wow, that doesn't bother you?" Young asked.

"No, all butterflies and moths feed on decomposing flesh. It is just rare to see." I looked at him. "Besides, I really like butterflies and moths. They are amazing creatures."

"I'm kind of horrified by that at the moment," Young answered.

"Let's take them back, scrape up all this as well," Xavier pointed to the shed floor.

"Done?" I asked.

"Well, I could request the collection of all the insects, but that would be a fool's errand." He grabbed the Monarch on my arm. Gently, he uncurled his fingers from around it. The monarch was uninjured. "However, it's unlikely they were poisoned, so..." He lightly breathed on the butterfly. It took flight, flittering away from us.

"To the morgue then," I suggested.

"My second favorite sentence in the world," Xavier answered.

Twelve

There is only so much a person can learn from three decomposed bodies and several bags of human goo. Xavier was currently gleaning every kernel of information he could from them. I was sitting on the counter, wondering if there was anyway the smell was ever going to come out of my hair. It may not have seemed like a big deal, but the truth was the smell could cling for days, and you got used to it. Once that happened, you didn't realize how badly you smelled.

Xavier had on his googly-goggles. They magnified his vision, which in turn, magnified his eyes when he was wearing them. It showed the small blood vessels that filled the whites of his eyes, feeding his optical nerve and pupil. The contrast of the red within the white was stark, making my eyes want to water in response.

The autopsies, if that's what they could be considered, were boring. The bodies were going to hold few, if any, real clues. The newest one had probably been in that shed for a month or more. The atmosphere had been conducive to a massive amount of insect activity.

Instead, I booted up a movie on my phone and let the sounds of Indiana Jones wash over the room. Xavier hummed along to the theme music as he did something terribly gross with the bags of human remains. I didn't hum along and I didn't watch him.

Indiana was in the middle of being offered monkey brains for dessert when something metallic clanked in the room. I couldn't resist, my eyes drifted to the stainless steel table where Xavier was sifting through the bags. There was a metal colander on the table that made my stomach flop. Xavier was staring intently at the table though. I tore my gaze away from the colander and looked at his googly-goggles.

Covered in gunk was an object about eighteen inches long with a heavy stone attached to one end. It didn't take a genius to figure out it was a necklace.

Xavier was carefully cleaning it with a solution that smelled a bit like hydrochloric acid and lemons.

I pulled on gloves. As soon as it was clean, I picked it up. It was definitely a necklace, gold box chain with a hematite pendant wrapped in gold wire. The wrapping was well done and the stone had a high polish on it. Craftsmanship went into the creation, there was no doubt about that. The chain was a mass produced chain, but the pendant wasn't. Someone had taken the time to hand wrap the wire. The marks of the pliers were visible if one looked close enough.

"Follow the pendant," I put the necklace aside. "Have you found anything else?"

"Does that look like a girl's necklace?" Xavier asked.

"It could be. Cassie buys stuff like this at craft fairs and festivals. She even takes the time to buy rough gems, clean them up, run them through a tumbler, and then polish them. She doesn't just buy it, she makes it."

"It's still weird that your niece enjoys doing that."

"My niece has her own Etsy store and makes money off it. Enough to pay taxes. She wants to design jewelry for a living. She's crafty like that." I tried to remember exactly what my mother had said a few days before I had left about it. Something Cassie had designed had recently sold for a lot of money because it was a rare mineral, but I didn't remember what, exactly. For some reason, it seemed important. My memory was amazing, except when it came to matters that involved my own family. Most of what they said went in one ear and out the other. I didn't mean for it to, it just happened.

"Fine, so this could be one of the girls'," Xavier said.

"Yep," I answered. "What do we know about them?"

"Cause of death is probably a single stab wound to the back that punctured the heart. However, I can only confirm that on one of them. They are all female. The youngest is probably twelve or thirteen. The oldest is seventeen to twenty, and she's been dead the longest. The first body was probably put in during the winter. The newest one was less than a month ago. The shed was sealed well, but very humid and warm. Given that we are in Texas, I'm not surprised about the heat; however, it hasn't been that warm for that long. The humidity raises some more questions, as it isn't that humid either. Yes, we've had a lot of rain, but not enough to account for this." He pointed to the bags.

"So, our bodies were melted on purpose?" I asked.

"That's what I think. I believe that before our killer used the shed, they fortified it, to some degree. There was no rodent activity, no raccoons or opossums sneaking in, just the insects. Once the third body was added, they somehow managed to pump up the heat and humidity in the room and start this process."

"A warm air vaporizer?"

"That would work. Only there wasn't any power."

"Lye, a warm air vaporizer, it's kind of strange, when you think about it. These are things they would do on a body farm, not in the middle of Texas. In the middle of Texas, a killer might use lye, but not a vaporizer."

"Someone watching how people decompose?"

"That would explain the lack of rage associated with the deaths. They came back to the place at least a couple of times."

"You're still thinking college student."

"It still makes the most sense." I shrugged. "It gives her access to her victims and it would instantly garner their trust. I'm sure there are smaller colleges than the University of Texas in Austin and San Antonio. Maybe they commute to school."

"We need some more identities," Xavier said, pulling off his gloves. Sweat covered his palms. I wrinkled my nose and did the same. "I've gone through the bags and there isn't much left of the bodies. It's up to Fiona at this point." He took digital pictures of the skulls and scraps of skin still clinging to them. Fiona had just gotten new software from MIT that was supposed to do digital facial reconstructions and attempt to match them to the missing persons' database. This was the first time it was being used. He hit the send button, and then shut down the digital camera with Wi-Fi capabilities. We had some of the best toys.

Having a serial killer plan ahead was one thing. Having a serial killer plan ahead so far that they were returning to the bodies months after their deaths to help with decomposition was completely different. Given that human goo almost never really dries and there was a lot of it found, it made me wonder just how many times the killer had returned. It also made me wonder how they managed to do it without smelling as if they were surrounded by decomposing corpses. Xavier and I leaving the morgue was proof that the smell clung to a person. People would grimace as we walked by; my hair would require multiple washes. Even then, the smell might hang around for a day or two.

The smell wasn't curable by Oust or air fresheners hanging from rearview mirrors. Febreze didn't take it out of clothes and hair, it didn't even cover up the smell. It just mixed with it, creating an even more oppressive smell.

There was another problem. We now had eight bodies. All of them young. None of them had been dead for more than two years, and none of them showed the uncertainties of a first time kill. Our killer might be local, but not all the bodies could be. Someone would have noticed. That was a lot for a town this size and high risk or not, they couldn't all have been declared runaways with no follow up. The very idea wasn't just illogical, it was ridiculous.

Our killer was importing victims. That was a nightmare. Catching a serial killer was sort of like playing roulette. You put your chips down and hoped luck was on your side. Most of the time, it is because serial killers are arrogant narcissists that like to show off. They had some patterns, some signatures, but it really was their attitude that they'd never be caught that got them caught.

Not this killer. She was all over the map. She was killing guys and girls. She was luring young teens as well as older teens to their deaths. She was experimenting with different ways to dispose of the bodies. The only thing that stayed the same was the cause of death and even that was questionable.

Perhaps there wasn't a single serial killing female at work in San Marcos. Perhaps there was a team or a trio. Perhaps, like Detroit, there was more than one and they were just crossing lines because the town wasn't really big enough for two serial killers.

It seemed unlikely that the three dead girls in the shed today were from a different killer, since at least one had in fact been stabbed through the heart.

Maybe one killer knew about the other and was dumping bodies in the same location. It was highly coincidental, but not unheard of. It had happened multiple times in California.

The notorious Interstate 5 that ran the length of the state of California was a serial killer's paradise. Towns are sparse, the road has several spots that are scenic outlooks, and there are some cell phone coverage issues. Starting in the 1970s, serial killers had been frequenting the interstate to both collect and dispose of victims. There were several instances of more than one serial killer working the interstate at one time. Since serial killers did in fact vary their victim preferences, methods of killing, and disposal methods from time to time, there were still victims that were only tentatively identified as belonging to a particular killer.

San Marcos was small, but it was a satellite for two larger cities with a major interstate running through it. However unlikely, it was possible that there was more than one killer working the stretch of road between San Antonio and Austin. With San Marcos being almost the center between the two places, it would be a good place for two serials to work and overlap without much suspicion, as long as they were importing most of their victims.

Austin had a population of nearly a million people. San Antonio was only slightly larger at one and a half million people. Our victim pool wasn't the measly fifty thousand that lived in San Marcos, it was the nearly two and a half million people that inhabited the area. More if we included other satellite towns and rural communities.

It also greatly increased our suspect pool. There wouldn't be a statistic for how many people had once lived in San Marcos and now lived in one of the other two cities, but it would be high. Kids would go to college in the larger places. They'd find jobs there after high school. Even if we limited the search to females between the ages of fifteen and thirty that had lived in San Marcos for at least one year, our suspect pool could easily be two or three hundred thousand people.

Another factor entered my mind. It was possible that the population of San Marcos increased on weekends. It was a small town with lots of seclusion, the perfect place for older teens to hook up with younger teens for a weekend of underage drinking. Relatives would travel back and forth to see each other. Just because someone lived in Austin or San Antonio wouldn't mean they would be unfamiliar with the area around San Marcos. Cousins liked to hang out together if they were roughly the same age. It was just a fact of life.

I sighed.

"What?" Xavier asked as we walked the half block from the makeshift coroner's office to the police station.

"I keep thinking of San Marcos as a small town and it isn't. It's a satellite town. The two are very different. Our suspect pool just became enormous."

"Do you ever have good news?"

"I co-own a puppy."

Thirteen

Upon arriving at the police station, Xavier and I were met with people holding their nose. We both ignored them. The walk had depressed him. If I had been capable of such an emotion, it probably would have depressed me too. Since I wasn't, I just felt tired. I wanted a hot shower with lots of soap. Tons of soap. I might have to go buy soap because I wasn't sure our hotel would be able to provide me with enough soap and shampoo to wash away the psychological aspects of human goo.

After twenty minutes of explaining why our victims couldn't all be from San Marcos and another twenty minutes explaining the concept of a satellite town and the migrant population, I flopped into a chair. Now, my entire team looked depressed, except

Fiona, who looked irritated. She'd identified a few of the victims. It supported my theory.

One was a local high school boy, but the others were from either San Antonio or Austin. The three new girls had yet to finish going through the software reconstruction. It would be tomorrow before we could start comparing their faces and body measurements to missing persons' reports. We had great toys, but they weren't always the fastest.

"Wow, what is that smell?" Ranger Young and Nails entered the room. Nails gave a small whine. Xavier and I held up our hands. We'd spent several hours sifting through decomposing humans. We could no longer smell it. "I was going to ask about dinner, but I think I lost my appetite."

"I want a shower," I told him. "A long one with enough soap to wash a herd of elephants. I want my clothes burned, that smell will never come out, and I want dinner." My stomach growled in agreement.

"Me too," Xavier nodded.

"Why don't you two go back to the hotel, get cleaned up, and rejoin us here," Gabriel said. "Well, maybe not in this particular room, we might need a new conference room while they sterilize this one."

"There isn't enough air fresheners in Texas to make this room smell better," Lucas informed us. "Normally, you guys smell bad after an autopsy, but this takes the cake."

"That reminds me, we think that our killer went back to our three young ladies in the shed to help speed up decomposition. We also think she sealed the room," Xavier said.

"You think?" Gabriel looked puzzled. It was rare for Xavier and me both to guess. Usually, the statement was "we know."

"Think," Xavier agreed. "There wasn't any evidence of chemical accelerant like with the well, but you don't always need chemicals. Bodies in hot, moist environments decompose faster than in dry or cool environments. Since it's May in Texas and not August in Texas, it seems unlikely that the decomp was completely natural, especially given the melting effect that we witnessed with the fatty tissues. The most likely culprit is a warm steam humidifier. However, that seems impractical, but we haven't thought of anything else that would do it."

"Which is why we smell so bad," I added for good measure.

"Aislinn's correct. Normal decomp is unpleasant, but when the fatty tissues melt, they release different chemicals than when they decay. The lack of scavenger activity coupled with the fatty tissue melting created bacteria-laden pools of brownish-black goo that was once a human being. That goo smells a lot worse than just a rotting corpse. Also, it has to be handled differently than solid matter, so we were essentially stirring it up, like stew boiling on the stove that gets the lid taken off and then stirred. It releases more odors," Xavier added.

"I think I'm going to be sick," Young sat down.

"It could be worse," I told him. "When encountering cannibals, most of the time, they are cooking. Some twisted cosmic joke or something. Anyway, a clean cannibal keeps his lair from smelling like decay, so instead, you smell things like roast and steak. The olfactory system triggers the hunger centers in the brain. You'll begin salivating and your stomach will rumble. Your brain knows you are smelling humans cooking, but your body just thinks of food. This system might not be triggered in hard-core vegetarians and vegans. I've never had one around to ask."

"What the, good Lord, I just, wow." Young said, stringing the unfinished thoughts into a single sentence.

"Yep, it's pretty gruesome on this side of the fence," Lucas told him. "Makes you wish you had gone into basket weaving or joined a punk band instead of becoming a law enforcement official."

"You guys do this every day?" Young said.

"Well, not every day. We get days off. For every three days spent on a case, we have to take one day off before we can move to another. So, if this case takes six days to wrap up, we'll have two days of zero serial killers before we return to duty. At least, most of us will. Aislinn will sit around reading true crime books while violent action movies play in the background," Gabriel said. "We've been at this for roughly thirty hours, we've earned one day off."

"Hey, hey," I interrupted. "It's not just violent action movies. I also enjoy British cop dramas and British comedies. I watch those while reading too."

"Do you have ADHD or something?" Young asked.

"No, her brain just doesn't work like ours," Fiona piped up. She was packing her equipment. "Aislinn's brain works at warp speed. She can't do just one thing at a time. It doesn't require enough brainpower, so she has to multitask. While she was helping Xavier in the morgue, I imagine she was also doing Sudoku problems and watching TV on her tablet."

"Indiana Jones on her phone," Xavier said. "No puzzles, she was busy mentally cataloging the amount of goo found to see if it was too much for three small females." I frowned at him. I had at one point been calculating that. Then he'd found the necklace and my brain started compiling facts about gold, necklaces, and hematite.

Xavier and I did what we were told. In the privacy of my own room, I put my clothing in a trash bag, tied it up, and set it outside the door of my hotel room. I noticed there was already a bag outside of Xavier's. Neither of us had been kidding about getting rid of the clothes. It was a pity really. It was one of my favorite T-Shirts that had the Black Knight from *Monty Python and The Holy Grail*.

Someone had been nice enough to give Xavier and me each several bottles of complimentary shampoo and multiple bars of soap when we stopped at the front desk.

Showers are interesting things for me. My brain never shuts off, literally. It is part of the reason I have trouble sleeping. At twenty-eight, I had been successfully bathing myself for more than two decades. It was automatic, mechanical, and required zero thought. Once in a great while, if I was exhausted or injured, I could shower and only do minimal thinking, but those times were rare. In a normal state, my mind kicked into overdrive the moment the water hit my skin, because my body and hair would get washed with no help from my brain.

Today was a normal day. As my hands emptied the second bottle of shampoo and began lathering up my hair again, my brain was in full swing.

Over a million people a year went missing. The most at risk age group was fourteen to eighteen. Even in the modern day, with cell phones carrying

GPS and the world revolving around debit cards, a person could still vanish without a trace. Some were no doubt dead, and their body just hadn't been found or identified yet, but not everyone who went missing could be dead. It was impossible to believe that the ten thousand serial killers at work in the US were each killing one hundred victims a year that we weren't finding, on top of the ones we were finding.

Of course, not everyone that was murdered was killed by a serial killer, but that still put the number of victims per killer every year at a staggering ratio.

One million plus people every year in a country that only held about three hundred million people was mind boggling. On top of that, we had roughly two hundred thousand a year murdered. Another two and a half million died of natural causes.

The only reason our population wasn't dropping was because people were breeding like rabbits. In the previous year, there had been just over four million babies born.

The Serial Crimes Tracking Unit arrested thirty-one serial killers and mass murderers per year, on average. The Violent Crimes Apprehension Unit did the same. This year, we would catch more than our average, because of our adventures in Detroit. However, it didn't seem like either of us was making much of a difference. For every serial killer we took out of the general population, there was one preparing to take the empty space.

Suddenly, I wondered if my work was worth it. The answer was yes, simply because if we weren't catching sixty or so serial killers a year, we'd be ears deep in them. No other law enforcement group was catching as many killers as we were. The number wasn't increasing, because we were catching them.

It wasn't causing a decrease in the number of people that went missing every year. There were other factors at work with the missing. Factors that I couldn't fathom. It was impossible for me to imagine someone just walking away and disappearing. Even though that was exactly what my grandfather had done.

My grandfather had beaten my grandmother to death, chopped her into small pieces, strung them throughout the house, and then disappeared into the ether. It turned out that he had been living under his brother's name in Nevada and making a very nice living as a construction contractor. He'd only come out of hiding to trim our family tree. That was something I didn't hold against him, our tree had needed some trimming.

Fourteen

I had contemplated The Missing for as long as possible. My skin had gone all pruny and white by the time I stepped from my shower. Dressing had been an easy affair, as I mostly wore jeans and T-shirts with a lightweight jacket to cover my guns when I was in public. The lax dress code for us was nice, and I would have hated to have to throw away a suit such as Malachi wore.

My T-Shirt had a chemistry joke on it. I couldn't remember the last time I had actually purchased a T-shirt for myself. People, particularly my team and Nyleena, picked up T-Shirts for me. Sometimes as gifts, sometimes just because they saw it and thought of me. It was a good thing, as I went through a lot of them. Between helping in the morgue, which could get fairly dreadful, and being injured, I lost one or two every time we went after a killer. Trevor disapproved of the constant T-Shirt wearing, comparing me to Xavier, but I never looked like I had slept in mine, so I ignored his complaints.

Dinner was held in a restaurant, a real one, not a chain. It was a mix of Tex-Mex and burgers. I could live with that and ordered quite a large meal. My stomach growled as I waited for my two enchiladas and two tacos to be delivered. I restrained from eating the chips and dip, or I'd get full on that and still force the enchiladas and tacos down my gullet.

Young had been invited to join us. Nails wasn't with him, which made me wonder if he lived close. I considered asking him, but that would open up more inquiries into my personal life.

Our cell phones all started going off about the time our food arrived. This meant more bodies had been found. I sighed and asked for a to-go box. My dinner companions did the same. Gabriel was the only one that bothered to read the text message.

"Good news, we can still eat at the police station," Gabriel put his phone away. "They had two teens reported missing tonight though."

"Missing teens," I frowned. I hadn't voiced my hair-brained idea that it might be a teen doing the killing. Killer teens weren't this organized. They didn't have the experience to plan ahead like our killer. Now, I was glad I had kept the thought to myself.

"Is it possible that Aislinn's theory of multiple killers is correct?" Xavier asked.

"Possible, yes. California's had as many as five serial killers on I-5 at the same time. Is it probable is the real question, and I-35 isn't I-5. There's a reason that road is notorious for serial killers; it's a good hunting ground. This interstate has too much traffic for that sort of behavior, so I'd say the probability is low," Lucas answered. "In other words, I refuse to give a firm answer on the matter. It could be multiples or it could be one. I've seen nothing to indicate more than one serial killer, but I also can't be sure, because most of the bodies are in an advanced stage of decomp when we find them. I do agree with her about the whole science fair technique being used to accelerate decomp. It is abnormal."

"Wishy washy psychobabble," I smiled at him. Lucas had issues. He didn't like to be called a profiler, but he was. There was no other way to put it, and the BAU would have loved him, if they were still capable of catching serial killers. Unfortunately, they were old school and to them, every serial killer was still motivated by a sexual urge and killers didn't just stop. The SCTU and VCU both worked on the basis that very few serial killers were sexually motivated, and that they did in fact, just stop, from time to time, for very long periods of time. The BAU still existed, but their role had changed drastically in the last decade and serial killers were not their primary focus anymore. They were more useful in determining acts of terrorism and whether it was homegrown or imported.

"Why are we going to investigate missing persons' reports?" Fiona asked.

"We aren't, we are going to listen in and see if we can figure anything out," Gabriel told her.

My food was lukewarm by the time I got the container open and began eating it. I was forced into a cramped room with too many people and not enough elbowroom. However, I was used to that. I wasn't used to trying to eat in the supply closet turned surveillance area. It made me wish that the interrogation rooms from TV were real. We could have pulled in folding chairs and sat like normal people as we watched through the one-way glass instead of attempting to glean tiny bits information from a small TV monitor with crappy speakers.

One was a sixteen-year-old girl. Sabrina Reeves had been missing since Wednesday. I was fairly certain that today was Sunday, although, there was the possibility that I was wrong. Even if I was a day off, she had been missing for a couple of days before her parents decided to report her. I was not a parent, nor would I ever be, however, my own experience had taught me that my parents had reported me missing within six hours. Perhaps it was my age or my father's profession, but it seemed like these parents had waited a very long time to file the report.

The other was a boy; he'd gone missing the night before. At seventeen, Shawn Steiger wasn't a high-risk runaway type. He was a good student with good grades. He'd last been seen at a party. From there, he had just vanished. Originally, his parents thought he might have slept over at the host's house, but when he had not returned by lunch, they had called. He hadn't slept over and no one had seen or heard from him since last night.

Since our killer had no gender preference, it was possible that one or both of them were now deceased. We really didn't know a time pattern, if one existed, so it was impossible to know if this was acceleration or just opportunity. For all we knew, our killer might be killing twice a week for the last four years and the city of San Marcos was not only stuffed with bodies, but the surrounding areas might be as well. There were too many variables and not enough constants to develop a good working theory.

I was not good with variables. I preferred constants. Mostly because I was not an investigator, I was an action taker. At this moment, I realized I was going to be interviewing high school students again. My last interaction with this special breed of humanity had happened in March, not counting my own family, which did not require interrogation. Their names were long forgotten, but I still remembered them as Ditzy and Dumb, high school seniors that had seen a man dumping bodies into a lake in Minnesota. I had wanted to Taser them both just to see if it would kick start their brain cells and stop them from saying, "like, you know."

The phrase had been popular in the 1980s and early 90s. It should have died a slow, quiet death as teens evolved into adults in the mid and late 90s. Apparently, it hadn't, at least not in Minnesota.

As I shoved the last bit of cold taco in my mouth, my phone rang. The caller ID proclaimed it was Malachi. The phone stopped ringing and a text message appeared before I could put it away.

Need you was all the text said. A few seconds later, it started ringing again.

"I'm busy," I answered in hushed irritated tones.

"You like to make jokes about werewolves in Wisconsin, what do you know about them in Ohio?" Malachi asked.

"Do you have a werewolf in Ohio?"

"Possibly; we have what appears to be a werewolf on the border of Indiana and Ohio."

"What part?"

"Northern area," Malachi said.

"Let me call you back, grab some silver bullets."

My parting shot to Malachi got me some looks from people in the room. I had mostly forgotten about them. Xavier grinned at me.

"Malachi having werewolf problems?" Xavier asked.

"He isn't ruling it out which, in itself, is sort of strange. Malachi doesn't believe in that kind of mumbo-jumbo," I answered.

"Why call you?" Young asked.

"Because the only thing Ace reads more of than true crime is case studies in the unexplained. She's pretty interested in preternatural and supernatural occurrences," Xavier answered for me.

I frowned at him. Not for answering the question so much as saying the words out loud. Everyone I knew was at least a little crazy. Malachi believed in UFOs visiting earth and mutilating animals. Nyleena believed there was a giant laser cannon in space. Gabriel had seen a wendigo. Lucas believed in ghosts and had seen them on more than one occasion, if you asked him about it. Fiona was a pagan who believed in magic. Xavier believed in demons and demonic possession. It was hard not to be interested in that sort of stuff.

My phone went off again. Another text.

How long?

Couple of hours probably. Read up on Dogmen of Michigan.

Not in Michigan.

Read it anyway. My fingers flew across the keyboard of my iPhone, typing as fast as Malachi responded. Ohio and Indiana both touched Michigan. However, I wasn't sure the Dogmen of Michigan qualified as werewolves. Sightings of them went back at least a hundred years, and Native Americans that inhabited that area had legends of the Dogmen that went back a lot further. However, if someone thought they were a Dogman, it was possible that they could outfit themselves with the proper gear.

At the moment, I was fighting with my brain. It was trying to recollect and spew forth everything it remembered about Dogmen, while I needed it to concentrate on listening to the interviews with the parents of the missing teens. While werewolves were interesting, they were not important, at least not to me, at the moment.

I crossed my arms over my chest and focused on the screen holding Sabrina Reeves' parents. They were currently explaining that she was often a runaway, so they hadn't immediately reported it. They had expected she'd be back in a few days. I sighed heavily.

"Currently wishing you were chasing suspected werewolves wherever Malachi is instead of preparing to interview teenagers that attended a party last night?" Xavier whispered to me.

I didn't answer. I did wish I were chasing suspected werewolves in Ohio and Indiana instead of preparing to interview partygoers. Life was brutally cruel sometimes.

Studying

Jess finished writing her paper after the party. Becky was only sort of helpful because she'd drank too much jungle juice to be a lot of help. She kept mumbling about red scarves and letters. Jess had decided to tuck her into bed and then studied for her advanced chemistry final.

Chemistry was one of her favorite subjects. The world of chemistry was a fascinating place. She could do without all the formulas and memorization of said formulas, but the rest of it was cool. It had helped her quite a bit in the last year. She'd learned about the corrosive properties of several household materials.

There was still two weeks of school left. She had finals in six of her classes. Most of them were this week. She had no idea what the point of the last week was. She wouldn't be learning anything. Seniors would be skipping classes, pulling pranks, and getting away with all of it. Their last hurrah before heading off to college or the service industry.

For those who were not seniors, the week would be spent having yearbooks signed and watching silly films. It was the prerogative of the teacher to decide how to spend the last week. A few of her advanced classes would probably give an overview of what next year would hold, but those were definitely the minority.

However, she understood that the teachers needed a week or so to grade finals, get them entered, and submit the grades to the school. Seniors would need to know if they had to attend summer school because of one stupid grade. Summer school would be tailored to meet the needs of the seniors.

Understanding it didn't mean she had to like it. Her summer would be busy. She would still have volleyball practices. She would be working in her mother's office part time as a file clerk. It would be her job to make sure all the charts were accurately filed, duplicate files would be merged, papcrwork from hospitals would need to be added, and any referrals her mother made would need follow up. When she wasn't doing that, she'd be entering immunization records, they were her mother's bread and butter during the summer, along with sunburns and insect bites.

It wasn't a glamorous lifestyle. Many people thought doctors took lots of vacations and drove expensive cars. Some did, but not her mom. Jess's mom worked long hours with overbearing parents and sensitive kids. Outside of work, her life consisted of Jess's volleyball games and Saturday night dates with her husband.

That was why Jess wanted to be a doctor. She wanted a simple life and she wanted to help people. Being a doctor would provide both, and if she were an ER doctor or a trauma surgeon, she'd have the touch of adrenaline that kept her happy.

Besides, success was a given in the family. Her older sister was in law school at Harvard. Her brother had gone to MIT and then joined the military. He did something that he couldn't talk about because it was highly classified. Jess couldn't imagine bucking the family tradition and doing something like running a daycare. Running a daycare was for silly women who couldn't pass real college classes. The kind that majored in art and squeaked by with a C.

It was why Jess studied so hard. She was going to be successful. She was going to graduate next year as valedictorian and have her pick of undergraduate schools. She was going to win scholarships for both meritorious work and volleyball.

It was also why Jess hadn't gotten as drunk as Becky at the party. Not only had she been the designated driver, but a minor in possession or a driving while intoxicated charge would not look good on her college resumes. She'd limited herself to just two cups of jungle juice.

Becky had been letting off steam. Not just from finals week, but from her father. Becky's father, William, was a world-class asshole. Technically, he was the town's mayor. He was serving his fourth term as such and he thought he owned the world as a result. He dictated everything Becky did to keep him from looking bad. Of course, that hadn't worked with his wife either, and she had left when Becky was young and William was serving his first term as mayor.

Jess was sure that William didn't care about Becky, except in her capacity to prop up his image. With Becky, he looked like a dedicated, hard-working family man, raising a daughter on his own. Most of the town was oblivious to the fact that Becky had pretty much raised herself, and when she'd needed a parent, she had gone to Jess's mom, not her own father.

Becky's determination was the part that Jess liked most about her. She was stubborn and determined, just like her. Jess felt protective of Becky; it didn't matter that Becky was a few months older. It was one of the reasons that Jess had considered killing William. Her family would take Becky in for senior year. The two girls were already as close as sisters were. Sharing a roof would only bring them closer. They were even talking about applying to the same colleges.

Jess sighed. She was running a little late on the application thing. She should have applied early, and she'd already taken both the ACT and SAT and scored really well on both. However, she was still hoping to improve in volleyball, so she had held off. Her parents never mentioned it to her, but she knew they had expected it. Her sister had done it. Her brother hadn't, but there had never been any doubt that he would be accepted to MIT. His seventh grade science project had been to build a power plant that combined wind turbines and solar panels. He'd used it to charge a car battery. Needless to say, the judges had been impressed.

Jess's seventh grade science fair project had not been as amazing. Although she had received high marks for her use of a subsonic sound to attract insects to a plant, a bee had stung one of the judges. It wasn't exactly the kind of impression she had wanted to make, but bees, especially Africanized bees, were unpredictable.

Suddenly, she struck on an idea. She shook her head, astounded that she hadn't thought of it sooner. She could install the subsonic insect attractant to Becky's house and wait for Africanized Bees to start building a hive. Texas was full of the deadly bees. It would only be a matter of time before they went after William. Becky would give them a wide berth if she knew they were there. William was dumb enough to prod them with a stick.

It would be a tragic accident. Even people not allergic to bees died from being attacked by a swarm of Africanized bees. William would think his position as mayor would keep the bees from stinging him. He was just that sort of person.

Jess would do it this summer. Her family was going on vacation in July for a week. They were going to visit her grandparents in Colorado. Her sister was supposed to meet them there. Becky was going too. Jess would just accidentally leave the attractant at Becky's. No one would think that Jess had meant to do it. She'd forgotten the contraption in the past and the school had needed to be shut down for a week while the exterminators worked to clear the bees.

She'd studied, written a paper, and solved a problem that had bugged her for a couple of years now. It was a productive night. Becky was snoring in the bed. Jess turned out the small desk lamp and snuggled up with her friend. Her friend gave a snort and settled back to sleep.

Jess listened to Becky's heartbeat. It was slow and steady. She counted the beats, concentrating on the sound of the other heart instead of the feel of her own. It took effort. It was a challenge Jess did every time Becky stayed the night. It helped her focus on the exterior parts of her life. That heartbeat was incredibly important to Jess. It helped keep her stable in moments that might otherwise have been problematic.

Plus, ignoring her own heart to listen to Becky's required concentration. It was a skill that Jess was honing. She wanted to be able to hear heartbeats other than her own, especially as they faded away. If she could feel that over her own beating heart, she would be able to conquer the world. Her own body being background noise to whatever was going on.

Fifteen

I slept, but I didn't sleep well. My dreams kept waking me, dreams of dead teenagers, stacked to the ceiling in a barn and smelling like flowers and decay because they had been covered with lavender essential oil.

It was my brain making connections between different types of funerary rites and historical events. In London, during the middle ages, cemetery space had been at a premium and more than one church had filled its cellars with the dead and attempted to cover up the smell. They could do little about the coffin flies that occasionally became aggressive towards living people. Those flies and the smell had put a stop to the practice. However, most of the bodies had been moved to the Thames for disposal. Not very ceremonial or hygienic. That was before the plague had happened and the invention of plague pits.

My day was going to be spent interviewing teens. Lucas had prepared a set of questions for me to ask. I couldn't browbeat or intimidate them. At least, I wasn't supposed to do that. That too was interfering with my sleep.

In theory, I should have been able to relate a little more with teens. Teens were very egocentric. They were immune to the dangers that stalked the world, at least, in their minds. They suffered from low impulse control and a lack of appreciation for extended consequences. Essentially, they were all sociopaths as they waited for their brain to finish developing.

I suffered these same problems, to an extent. My intelligence and the network of Jiminy Crickets I had developed in recent years kept me from behaving like a full-blown sociopath. Life was like a game of chess to me and each action was weighed before being taken, if I had the time. When I was in foreign moral territory, I turned to Nyleena or someone similar for advice.

My body struggled to go back to sleep, but my mind was determined it needed to be kept awake. It just couldn't remember why. I shined the flashlight from my phone on my toes and wiggled them. I hadn't stretched for a day or two, and I could feel it in my legs. Catching sight of my pajamas reminded me of what I was supposed to do. The pants had puppies napping on chew bones and said "bone tired." It was almost dawn according to my phone, and Malachi would be awake.

"It's about time," he snapped at me.

"I forgot, I have my own serial killers to chase," I informed him. "So, do you really believe your suspect is a werewolf, or is it a person pretending to be a werewolf, or is it a person suffering a delusion that he's a werewolf?"

"Our biggest clue is wolf hair found on all the victims and he's taking chunks out of them with his teeth. However, he doesn't have normal teeth, he has fangs. A double set on both top and bottom based on the bite marks."

"There are cases of people wearing wolf pelts and attacking people because they believed the pelts made them werewolves. The most famous was the werewolf of somewhere in France. He was hanged, but went to his grave proclaiming to be a werewolf. The area you're in does have legends of Dogmen. Sightings are mostly by townsfolk, which is sort of weird, but the native tribes in that area believed that a race of Dogmen lived in the area. Strangely, werewolf sightings are not that uncommon. People are more inclined to see werewolves than any other mythical being with the exception of Bigfoot. There are plenty of documented cases of people with mental illnesses proclaiming to be werewolves. Talk to fetish clubs that specialize in blood play. They will know if one of their members has a set of dentures to fit the mold. They'll also know if anyone likes to dress up as a wolf. Unfortunately, lycanthropy is indeed, a sexual fetish and if he has started killing, it's because he isn't getting the release from sex that he used to."

"What about the Dogmen?"

"I've never met one, but if you do, they don't conform to European werewolf myths. They die like normal people; a few bullets to the head will do the trick."

"What kind of killer are you chasing?"

187

"The kind that kills teenagers. I actually get to spend the day interviewing them. So excited."

"Don't kill any of them," Malachi hung up. I dressed and read a book while waiting to start the day. I had grabbed one on killer teens. It was confirming my theory. Killer teens were disorganized. They were filled with emotion, which also meant the crime scenes were covered in blood. Even the most thought out crime by a teen had included slitting the throat of his victims. His forethought had been to stand behind the victims, minimizing the amount of blood he got on himself. However, it was also just easier to slit someone's throat from behind, so that wasn't necessarily done because he was thinking about blood spatter.

Armed with some new information about serial killers, I was almost ready to tackle the task ahead. We wouldn't find our serial killer among the partiers, unless there had been someone older there, but maybe we would get a lead.

"Last time I saw Shawn he was looking for Becky." The sixteen-year-old gum chewer said between bubbles. I desperately wanted to choke the shit out of the little brat. The gum was annoying.

The answers were unhelpful. The witness was worse than most. He was obviously still a little drunk.

"When was that?" I asked for the third time.

"I dunno, after dark. He spent some time talking to another girl, her name is Jessie, and then he went looking for Becky," the kid answered, yet again. Each time he added onto what was happening, but he seemed oblivious to the existence of clocks on the planet.

"You didn't check your phone at any time during the party or a clock?" I huffed.

"Sure, I got text messages all night. I have to keep up with the ladies. I got a booty call about midnight and left around two. I went to Marsha's, got off, then went home and crawled in bed, which is where I was when my parents told me I had to come here."

"Did you see Shawn around the time you got one of these text messages?"

"Nope."

"Here's the deal," I finally snapped. "You are going to drink several bottles of water, spit out the gum, and we are going to try this again when you've sobered up a little."

"Does that mean I get to go home?"

"No," I slammed the door behind me. I should have kept the clothes. I could have left them with the gum chewer for a while. Maybe if he vomited uncontrollably for several hours, he'd be sober enough to figure out his buddy was in serious danger of being dead.

"Getting anywhere?" Lucas asked.

"Nope. What the hell is wrong with teenagers?"

"You were a teenager once. You don't remember what it was like?"

"Lucas, I do not believe my time as a teenager is comparable to other teenagers. I did not get invited to parties. I did not crash parties. I did not even have many friends. I was not just a social outcast, I was non-existent. I did not like teenagers when I was one. They were immature and brain dead."

"Teenage brains..."

"Stop, I don't care," I told him. "The physiological and psychological status of teenagers is more abhorrent than watching grass grow. I feel like my own ability to think is dampened by their disconnected reality. Dissociative disorders have a greater grasp on reality than a teenager."

"Cassie included?"

"Cassie included. She talks about boys, a lot. She drinks alcohol. She has sex. She's relatively normal, and I cannot connect with her as a result. Sometimes, there's a spark in the pan and I think we make a connection, but those are few and far between and possibly, completely unreal. I feel like I'm in a soap opera; Shawn liked Becky, Becky likes Matt, Matt likes Liz, Liz does not like Matt, she plays softball, like that means anything to the killings. Who cares if Liz likes softball, our killer isn't using a softball."

Xavier giggled, softly at first and then they overwhelmed him. The high pitched madman's giggle that creeped people out. I stared at him, daring him to continue. I had not said anything funny. Gabriel was smirking, so I glared at him instead. He looked away.

"Um, Ace, that's a polite way of saying that Liz is most likely a lesbian," Lucas told me.

"So, Liz doesn't like Matt because Liz is more likely to have a crush on Becky," I nodded. "It's a frucking soap opera. When did softball player become a euphemism for lesbian? Why not just say Liz likes girls? Why tell me she plays softball?"

"There is a stereotype that all female softball players are lesbians," Lucas said.

"That's dumb," I sighed. "How many are left to be interviewed?"

"None," Gabriel said. "We've interviewed everyone. No one remembers Shawn leaving. No one remembers anything unusual. He just vanished at some unknown time."

"Can I still force this kid to drink a bunch of water and stay in the room until he grows a brain?" I asked.

"Technically, no. He answered the questions, in his own way, like everyone else, he can't pin down the time he saw Shawn because he was drinking. Unfortunately, we can't charge them with underage drinking," Gabriel said. "The locals can, but won't, because too much time has elapsed and they weren't caught in the act."

"Unless you want to consider him a suspect in something other than teenage drama," Lucas teased.

Sixteen

Young was standing too close to me. I could hear his heart beat over my own. It was beating harder and faster than mine was. His breathing was shallow and unsteady. My own was working at a very slow fifty-five beats per minute, and it wasn't working hard to do it. Young's was closer to a hundred and twenty beats per minute. His pulse made his neck jump as his heart pushed the blood through his veins.

Nails was sitting in front of a barn door. I didn't need him to tell me that I was about to find another body or three. I could already smell it. The air was ripe with the scent of decay. Whatever was behind the door wasn't in the advanced stages of decomp. The smell still had a tang to it, meaning the body was fresh.

Neither Young nor I had moved towards the closed door. I was fine with finding bodies. I just wasn't sure Young was up for it. He worked mostly with Search and Rescue, not serial killer victim hunting. Even a victim that wasn't beaten to a pulp or partially eaten was considered awful simply because they had died at the hands of another human being. I had no idea why the human brain made the distinction, but Lucas had pointed it out to me on several occasions. Now, my mind had just accepted that it was worse to find a murder victim than someone who got lost in the woods and died of exposure.

"When you get ready, I'll go in first," I reassured him. We didn't have anyone else with us today. No one had wanted the job of tagging along with me, except Young and Nails. I was pretty sure Young had thought we wouldn't find a second set of victims. Nails didn't seem to mind. Young swallowed loudly.

"Go ahead," he finally said.

I walked up to the door. Nails looked at me, as if expecting a treat. I didn't have one for him and I didn't know if he was allowed treats anyway, so I

194

ignored him. In many ways, I understood dogs better than humans. I still wasn't the pet type, but dogs were simple to understand. They wanted love, approval, food, and a comfortable place to sleep, especially when it was raining or cold. Humans wanted a lot more than that and they were subtle about it. I had never learned the art of understanding subtle clues.

The door worked on a pulley system. It opened and the smell increased. Nails sat still. I frowned. With the door open, I could smell something else, something that wasn't human. Wet fur or hair was mixed with the scent of decay.

Nails was right, there was a cadaver in the barn. There were actually two of them. A horse that had been in the process of giving birth and a foal. They were both very dead.

"Horses," I shouted to Young. He timidly walked into the building. From several feet away, he craned his neck to peek into the stall, as if there was a chance I had lied to him. The problem wasn't the manner of death, as that was evident. The problem was that people tended to keep a close eye on animals giving birth in their care, particularly larger animals like horses and cows. They were worth a lot of money. Letting the mare and foal die was costly. We were also in a large barn with no other animals. It seemed a little strange to me. The house was abandoned.

Nails gave a loud bark. I drew my gun without thinking. Young jumped.

"Hallo?" A man's voice with a thick accent entered the stagnant air in the barn. My guess was that Nails was keeping him outside.

"US Marshals Service, Serial Crimes Tracking Unit," I shouted back. "Come around the corner, slowly." I took a position against the stall.

"The dog won't attack?" The voice asked.

"No," Young found his voice, but it had a slight tremble in it.

A man in his seventies or eighties shuffled around the corner. His hands were in the air. He looked very tired.

"Do you have identification?" I asked.

"Yes," the man slowly reached for his wallet and threw it at my feet. I kicked it to Young. Nails entered the barn.

"Edgar Barnes," Young told me.

"You live around here, Mr. Barnes?"

"I do, my house is just across the field."

"Are these your horses?" I asked.

"Unfortunately," he sighed, "I was in the hospital part of last week and the mare gave birth while I was there. My grandson was supposed to be watching out for them, but he forgot. I haven't gotten around to disposing of them yet." He wore a bandage around his leg. It was barely noticeable through the pant legs of his overalls. "The vet was going to do it, but he's had other matters to attend to, I guess."

"What happened to your leg?" I asked.

"Snake bite," Edgar Barnes shook his head. "Damn silly thing to do. I wasn't watching where I stepped and was struck by a rattlesnake. I managed to get help, but it put me in the hospital for four days."

I holstered my gun and gave the barn one last quick glance. I didn't notice anything out of the ordinary.

"Why don't we go outside, where the air is a little fresher," I told him.

"Sure," he shrugged as if he didn't smell it and maybe he didn't. Age was funny about things like that. Young seemed relieved. Nails sniffed the stall and then walked out ahead of us.

Once outside, I shut the barn doors. They clacked against each other. The smell receded some. Aside from Young's vehicle, which was clearly marked as being a police vehicle with a canine, there were no other vehicles. Edgar Barnes must have walked the field as he'd done countless times before. I'd met men like him before. Men who wouldn't give up and kept going, regardless of what was wrong with them. This brought my grandfather to the forefront of my mind and I had to push the thought away. Maybe they hadn't gotten all the tumor.

"Mr. Barnes, have you noticed anything unusual lately?" I asked.

"Not really; my grandson seems to have his head up where the sun don't shine, but otherwise, everything's been normal." He thought for a moment. "Except the dead kids they keep finding. Is that why you're here?"

"Yes," I answered. "Considering the location of where the first bodies were found, we are checking out properties that aren't located near any houses or anything. Hence, my looking in your barn."

"He's a good for nothing," Edgar spat on the ground. It was black. He was chewing and very good at hiding it. Normally, I noticed things like that, but to look at him or listen to him speak, one would never have known.

"Who, sir?" Young asked. I already knew the answer. The mare had been a Belgian, a workhorse, probably used to steer livestock.

"My grandson, but he's about the only family I got left. So, I reckon I have to live with that, but he's still worthless."

"How old is he?" I asked.

"Thirty-two, can't find a job, can't keep a woman, and can't drive a car without wrecking it. I think he's on drugs, but his mother disagrees. So, I keep my mouth shut about it. I don't need my daughter-in-law cutting ties with me. She's the only other family left."

"Why didn't she check on the horses?" I asked.

"Wheelchair," Edgar said. "She and my son were driving back from San Antonio one night and hit a cow that had gotten loose. Killed my son, paralyzed her. Terrible thing."

199

"I'm sorry to hear that," I told him. "So, what did you herd with that big mare?"

"Nothing anymore. She was the last one I had. Sold all my cattle about ten years ago and most of the horses, but I kept her mother and father. Her mother was a beaut, just like her. Couldn't bring myself to sell her mother or her, once she was born. I imagine her foal would have been just as pretty."

"Quite likely. Why don't we help get rid of the horses for you?" I offered. My father had been a cop, my grandfather a serial killer, but a lot of my family had been cattlemen. Horses and cattle just went together. Even in the early stages of decomp, she was a pretty mare. Her foal would have been worth a great deal to a horse breeder. Belgians weren't known for their agility, but they were even tempered and didn't spook easily. They were good, hard workers.

"That would be mighty nice of ya. With this bum leg, I'm having some difficulties running any equipment."

"So, what are you doing now that you aren't in the cattle business, Mr. Barnes?" I asked as we started walking through the field.

"Gettin' bit by rattlesnakes," he gave me a wink. I couldn't help but smile. Young and Nails followed. Nails seemed pretty happy with the situation. Young didn't. However, I wasn't going to leave an old man in need when I could help him. "Got an old John Deere, have ya ever run one?"

"Yes sir," I answered. "What model?"

"A 5020," he said.

"Wow, that is an old Deere, but I can run it." I assured him. One of my great uncles had owned a 5020, it was from the 1960s. He had refused to upgrade to a newer tractor because it did everything he wanted.

Seventeen

"Aislinn Cain, US Marshal, sociopath, serial killer expert, and philanthropist," Xavier said as Young and I entered the police station. Word of my work for Mr. Barnes had obviously gotten back to the police station.

"It was a simple matter of putting a horse in a pasture to decompose and be scavenged," I told him.

"Oh no, it was not. It was a matter of driving a tractor older than I am to move said horse to pasture," Xavier teased.

"Surely my Missouri roots did not escape your notice. I've driven tractors in the past. I've driven that exact model of tractor as a matter of fact."

"I just can't picture you on a tractor," Xavier squinted at me. "I mean, you just don't seem the farming type."

"Keep laughing it up, see if I don't Taser you," I said.

"You did a good deed, don't feel embarrassed about it," Xavier said.

"Name one time when I have been embarrassed."

"Good point. Aside from dead horses, did you find anything useful?" Xavier asked.

"If I had, I would have called you. Anyone else have any luck?"

"No," Lucas shook his head.

"How much of this blasted county have we searched?" I asked.

"Not even a quarter of it." Gabriel informed me as he put fresh maps on the table. "Fiona found matches for the girls you found yesterday. They all disappeared from San Antonio and one was only thirteen."

There was a lot of disparity between our victims. That really bothered me. It didn't matter that serial killers rarely followed their patterns all the time, but it was that this pattern was a like for teen girls and an understanding of chemistry. Chemistry was incredibly useful to killers. A serial killer with an understanding of chemistry could dispose of bodies, make bombs, and more effectively remove evidence.

"A park ranger just found a body, they want you," a cop stuck her head in the door. She immediately exited.

We followed in our standard issue black SUV with tinted windows. Young was ahead of us. Nails could be seen through the tinted back window. Maybe co-owning a dog would turn out to be a good thing. I texted my mother.

The declaration that a park ranger had found a body was a bit of a stretch. The park ranger had sort of found a body. The usual peppermint balm wasn't needed, the smell in the air was not of decomposition. It was hard to describe. It was acrid and stung the eyes, making them water. It made the nose burn and no amount of balm was going to help.

There was a liquid-like substance in a huge puddle on the dark, hardwood floor. Burn marks ran away from the puddle in long trails. The floor near the puddle was becoming spongy and my feet sank a little as I stepped on what used to be solid wood.

One side of the body was more recognizable than the other with only a few holes and burns to the flesh. A single brown eye stared blindly at the ceiling. The other was part of the liquid substance on the floor. I kept far enough back to keep it from getting on my shoes. I wasn't sure it would eat the soles, but it might.

"I won't know for sure until I get a facial enhancement, but I'm fairly certain we just found Shawn Steiger," Xavier announced.

"What does that to a person?" A uniformed officer asked. He was a bit green in the face.

"Sulfuric Acid," Xavier and I said in unison.

"Isn't that a regulated substance?" The lead detective asked.

"Yes," I answered, "all acids are regulated. However, that's kind of misleading. When was the last time you had to sign to buy a gallon of good drain cleaner?"

"Never," the detective answered.

"And yet, the primary ingredient in really good drain cleaners is sulfuric acid. Not Drano or Liquid Plumber, those both use lye, because lye is great at eating through fats. They are not as effective if the clog is made of materials other than fats, like toilet paper. Sulfuric acid works by breaking down most biological materials, including cellulose, the main component in toilet paper and wood," I looked at the floor. "It also becomes more corrosive when mixed with water. A couple gallons of that, the tissues and hair are dissolved very quickly. It will eventually eat through the calcium in the bones as well, but that takes longer. Our killer was very sloppy with the drain cleaner, which is why half the face is still intact along with the limbs."

"In other words, next time you flush your daughter's pet goldfish down the drain, pour in a little drain cleaner made from sulfuric acid afterwards to keep the bones from mixing with toilet paper and creating a clog," Xavier explained.

"Does that happen?" Young asked.

"More than you think," Xavier answered. He looked at the floor. "I'm going to need the floor taken up for processing. We'll need a HAZMAT team to extract the body as well as the floor."

"It's still eating the remains?" The detective asked.

"Yep," Xavier said, "the floor is spongy, so it is still destroying the cellulose inside of the wood. There has really been nothing to neutralize it and I don't feel like we should contaminate everything by dumping several hundred boxes of baking soda on it."

"Hey," I pointed to the throat of our victim. All the tissue had been dissolved and only the bones were visible. The sulfuric acid was already working on the bones, as they were already becoming discolored. There were a few nicks on the hyoid bone as well as the spine behind it.

"I'm going to need at least one box of baking soda," Xavier said. In adults, the hyoid bone was one of the strongest bones in the body. In children and teens, it had yet to completely ossify. It was soft enough that the sulfuric acid wouldn't have the same difficulty dissolving it as other bones in the body. The nicks were unlikely to be from the acid, but it was evidence that we could lose at almost any time due to the lack of ossification.

Someone came up to Xavier with a box of Arm & Hammer. I raised an eyebrow, trying to figure out who carried baking soda in their car. Xavier slipped on gloves, removed the hyoid, and dropped it into the box. With his fingers holding the top flaps in place, he gave it a few good shakes, embedding the bone in the baking soda.

Looking at the hyoid bone reminded me of the necklace. We had names; we could identify the owner or discover if it belonged to the killer. There seemed nothing of real value in the abandoned station except Shawn Steiger.

I stood up and walked the open area. The wood was firm. The windows were gone from one wall. A rack was built into the wall. Leaves littered part of the floor, leftover from sometime. Inexplicably, there were bits of glass mixed in with the leaves. It almost looked like the leaves and glass had come in at the same time. The rest of the room didn't seem touched by weathering.

A small armadillo ran from behind the counter towards a back room. It was small enough that it still belonged to a mother. My guess was that they both lived inside the building. My feet followed it, as if I could interrogate the armadillo and find out information about our killer.

The back room was in disarray. Papers had been left in a closet, animals had scattered them about the space. Something hissed at me. A large, black cat had the small armadillo cornered and didn't want me muscling in on its meal.

Armadillos were carriers of leprosy and a few other diseases. Not that this was the armadillos fault. Nature needed animals to carry diseases and pass along to others, to ensure that balance and order was kept.

The cat hissed at me again. If the cat had been in here long enough, it could have killed the armadillo's mother. The thing would die regardless of whether I interfered or not. The cat didn't have a collar, but it was still at a healthy weight. I decided not to leave the armadillo at the mercy of the predator. I pushed the cat away with my foot and picked up the armadillo.

The shell was still soft. The claws weren't very long. It made a strange screeching noise that made me reconsider my decision to save it. Once I had hold of the armadillo, I snatched the cat by the back of the neck, yanking its feet from the ground. The cat made even worse noises, yowling and hissing as it attempted to kick its feet and gain control of its dangling body.

Lucas rushed into the room. He stood in the doorway and watched me for a moment, saying nothing. I'm not sure there was anything to say. There wasn't any blood visible in the room.

"Material witnesses," I told Lucas as I handed him the yowling predator. I kicked at some of the papers, still looking for blood. If the cat had eaten the armadillo's family, there would be remains somewhere. Armadillos never strayed far.

"You realize they build burrows, right?" Lucas asked.

"Yes, and carry leprosy. Would you prefer to hold him?"

"Leprosy aside, that animal is too young to live without a family."

"Well, I don't know any animal rescue places in Texas and the ones in Kansas City aren't going to come here for an armadillo. Having said that, the cat was going to eat it and I wasn't sure that was exactly the right thing either. He's fat and healthy."

"One less armadillo isn't going to put a strain on the ecology of the region."

"Perhaps not, but I still wasn't going to let the cat eat it." There were no signs of armadillo inhabitation within the building. There was definitely evidence that the cat had been living there for a while.

"So, you're almost normal again."

"In this case, the cat is no different than a serial killer. It can go to a home, it doesn't have to eat the armadillo."

"Black cats are the hardest cats for a shelter to adopt out. Too many superstitions surrounding them."

"Bleach spots into his fur. They do it with dogs," I said.

Lucas gave a quick laugh, shook his head and walked out. I frowned. What the hell was I going to do with an armadillo?

Eighteen

Shawn Steiger's last day on earth had not been a very good one. His stomach contents had included chicken contaminated with salmonella. He'd knocked his leg on something, probably a coffee table, which had left a nasty black bruise on his shin. His toe was broken around the same time and was roughly the same shade of black as the bruise. If he hadn't been murdered, he would have had several weeks of misery ahead of him.

Xavier had found a large quantity of alcohol in his system. Not falling down drunk, but he wouldn't have been thinking clearly. I remembered what that idiot Simon had said; he'd gotten a booty call. I was fairly certain this meant he'd gotten called by someone who wanted to have sex, but I hadn't Googled it yet for final confirmation.

The same could have happened to Shawn. Having such a crappy day, if someone had offered him sex, he probably would have been overjoyed. However, he wouldn't have known about the salmonella poisoning yet. A broken toe and banged up shin was still grounds for a bad day. Most likely, he willingly left the party with his killer or he left to meet her.

I was under no illusions about the sexual activities of teenagers. It always surprised me how many people really believed that teen sex had only started in the last few decades. Teens have been jumping in and out of bed with each other since the beginning of time. The biggest change was our perception of it. Aside from the upper class, teens were usually married by age sixteen. The upper class kept their girls from marriage a little longer, but they were engaged by seventeen or in some cases, a year or two earlier. It was just the marriage that was delayed. Hell, in some cultures, as soon as a girl started menstruation, they were of marriageable age.

Our modern day morality had swept this under the rug, proclaiming teens should be abstinent until marriage and using history as its example, while quietly ignoring the fact that the majority of teens were indeed married. I was sure that Cassie was sexually active. I hoped that she used condoms and did not send out booty calls.

Then again, the day had been full of people not having good days. One of our three female victims had also been having a very bad day before being murdered. According to the parents of Esperanza Cortez Pena, she'd gone to a store to buy a computer and other items, as their house had been burgled the day of her death. At some point, heading to the store, her car had broken down. It was at this time that she had met her killer. It had also been Esperanza's seventeenth birthday.

Tina Little was our thirteen year old. She was active in soccer and her church. She was always doing something to help with local charities. Her grades were average. Her parents were average. Her life was average. Stranger danger aside, Tina was not high risk for anything except a medal for community service.

Liberty Kent, the third victim, had been eighteen. She had just graduated high school the year before and was working two jobs. Her goal was to save enough money to get an apartment the following year and start attending a community college. Like Tina and Esperanza, she was not high risk.

Greg Johnson had been six feet six inches tall the day he went missing from San Marcos. He was a basketball player and by all accounts, a steroid user. He was our biggest outlier. His size and physical abilities might explain why his killer had sliced through his Achilles' tendon.

Angela Schmidt had been twenty and a college student at the University of Texas. Her roommate claimed she suffered a touch of obsessive-compulsive disorder. She wrote all her papers out longhand then typed them, twice. The other big issue, according to her roommate, was being the first person to class. She always left early, but if she were the first one there, she would stand outside in the hall until someone else had taken a seat. She also couldn't be later than tenth to sit down or she would skip class. On her last day, she had gone missing after her last class of the day. She'd made plans to meet her roommate and two other girls at a restaurant near campus, but she had never shown up.

Nathan Jones had definitely been high risk. Hopefully, life for his little sister would be better now that I had kicked their father's ass. It would be tragic for their mother to lose both children.

Gail Vincent had also been from Austin, but she had been a junior high student. At the tender age of fourteen, she was in foster care. Her parents had abused and neglected her. They'd even pimped her out to pedophiles. Since she entered the system a year earlier, she'd run away twice. Her maternal grandparents lived in New York. She'd never met them, but her only prized possession had been a postcard from them dated before she was born. It had been her goal to find them. Calling her high risk was like saying that anteaters had claws.

Shawn Steiger had not been high risk. Exactly the opposite, in fact. He had been a good student, a member of the student council, and a senior who had been accepted to Yale. He'd lived in the exact same house all of his life. His parents were devastated by his death.

Our final victim was Bonnie Turner. She was sixteen, no record, good grades, but not really a joiner, she didn't belong to any clubs or play any sports. She was shy, quiet, and taking meds for anxiety. Her father had died in a freak accident when she was nine and she'd had some problems with agoraphobia ever since. He had been beheaded while trimming a tree. The rung of the ladder he was standing on broke and he'd fallen on the running chainsaw, cutting his own head off. Bonnie and her older brother, Cameron, had been holding the ladder.

The missing persons' summary sheet for each of the victims did reveal a tiny spark of information. None of them was short. Not just not short for their age, but average by adult standards. Even the two young victims were at least five feet, four inches tall.

The frown appeared on my face without my approval. I could feel the corners of my mouth turning down, wrinkles were forming on my forehead, and my eyes were narrowing. I sighed, trying to get rid of the frown, but that just made me frown more.

"Our killer is diminutive," I announced. Everyone turned to look at me. The conference room had been quiet right up until I opened my mouth. "Look at the descriptions of our victims. They were tall and even if they weren't playing sports, they weren't thin or incredibly overweight, but they were within the average weight for their height. How does a girl with OCD disappear? Or a girl who battles agoraphobia? They must have felt completely secure with their killer. The only thing that explains it is age and stature. None of them perceived her as a threat. So, either our killer knows the Vulcan Death Grip or she poses as someone very non-threatening. Most people equate physical stature with physical capabilities. Bonnie Turner wouldn't have trusted a woman who was taller than she was, she was being treated for anxiety. Anxiety disorder means everything is a potential hazard. Her killer was not only non-threatening, but somehow reassuring." That little voice in my head whispered to me. I ignored it.

"Like little person diminutive?" Gabriel asked.

"No, that's too short. I'm thinking someone who is below average height and possibly, weight," I said. "Think about it. Why cut the Achilles' heel? Why was the hyoid bone struck by the blade, but the ribs haven't been? She's short. Shawn was probably bending into her when she stabbed him in the throat. Greg Johnson had a nick on his rib from the blade, but he was six feet six inches tall. That's tall, even by modern standards."

"Ok, a short serial killing med student or anatomist. That shouldn't be hard to find," Lead Detective Mark Skartal said. I didn't know where Hight had gone, but I missed him at the moment. Skartal was shaping up to be a jerk.

"Your sarcasm is noted," I snipped at him. I considered Tasering him, but in a police station in Texas, this seemed like a really bad idea. I didn't think they would be as nice as the sheriff's department in Anchorage, Alaska. "Also, that hematite necklace was not identified as belonging to any of our victims. I do not believe it was just lying around in the shed while the bodies of three young women decomposed into puddles. Somehow, it got tangled up and dropped by the killer. Hematite is not expensive, but I believe the gold wire is. It is high quality jewelry wrapping wire. I'm sure the lab report will tell us that it is eighteen karat. I'm thinking a local artisan made it, unless it was purchased off a small artisanal website or Etsy, which would be awful, because it's unlikely to be traceable."

"How many people work with hematite and gold?" Skartal asked.

"Hundreds, maybe thousands of small artisanal jewelers," Lucas answered for me. "It's big business to have one of a kind pieces of jewelry these days."

"Even my sixteen year old niece is working with the stuff. She has an Etsy store and makes several thousand a year off it, all on jewelry," I said, ignoring that stupid voice again.

Nineteen

My phone had vibrated itself off the table several minutes earlier. The bright screen flashed to life once again as the contraption danced across the carpet. My phone case was black, but even with only a single light out, the shadow could be made out.

At the moment, I was trying to figure out a way to explain why I thought our serial killer was small in stature. Even Lucas had seemed unsure about it. Malachi's werewolf would have to wait. I didn't have time to discuss the philosophical aspects of a person who believed they could shapeshift.

To me, the theory made sense. Smaller people were just less intimidating, unless I knew the person was suffering from either ASPD or borderline personality disorder. Furthermore, if I knew it to be borderline, I was still less intimidated by a smaller person.

I was a good example. I was a few inches shorter than the national average of five feet, five inches tall and I weighed about one hundred and thirty pounds. I was evenly proportioned, legs to torso and all of that made me unimpressive to look at. When I could manage a real smile, I was capable of disarming most people. That was my flaw though, not the flaw of a pure psychopath, who could be charming when it served their purpose, even achieving real smiles with the flip of a switch.

Should a psychopath be a few inches shorter than I was and a dozen or so pounds lighter, they would be well camouflaged. She would appear to be too small to be dangerous and too friendly to be anything but sincere.

That did of course depend on the type of psychopath. Studies on female psychopaths were still rare, because female psychopaths were still rare. To make it worse, the majority of female psychopaths had Borderline Personality Disorder, not Anti-Social Personality Disorder. Borderlines didn't have the genetic mutations that went with ASPD. They also tended to be more violent for longer periods of time.

With that in mind, our killer was exhibiting the traits associated with ASPD psychopathy and not Borderline. That meant she was a whole lot closer to having my mentality than the females that had been studied. The thought was cringe-worthy.

The distinction between nature and nurture was becoming more and more evident with the rise of the abnormal personality. I was sure Lucas occasionally scribbled notes about me before he went to bed. I was his own personal case study. I wasn't just a female psychopath with ASPD, but I had somehow managed to exchange some of the psychopathic personality traits with sociopathic personality traits. The jury was still out about whether this was a help or a hindrance. Until recently, I had always considered it a good thing, but recent events were making me rethink that.

Using myself as the model for our serial killer, two things became crystal clear. She was very smart and she was much better with the camouflage. Proving this to my team members was difficult.

Proving it to people who didn't know me was damn near impossible.

My phone began vibrating again. I picked it up. Malachi's number flashed across the screen for the hundredth time.

"I'm thinking," I snarled into the receiver.

"I've been reading up on people who suffer from lycanthropy, the mental disorder, not the actual werewolf thing."

"So?"

"So, they may be out of my league."

"I'm on a case."

"I know. I'm not asking you to drop everything and come here. I need some more advice."

"Lycanthropy as a mental illness is pretty straight forward. For whatever reason, the person thinks they are a werewolf."

"Yes, I read all that. What I am trying to figure out is how to identify someone who thinks they are a werewolf."

"Look for the normal signs; baying at the moon, running around naked, hunting for rabbits on all fours."

"As far as I can tell, they don't do that."

"I have no idea. I've never actually encountered a werewolf or someone who thinks they are one. Lycanthropy is a fairly rare mental illness. Have you checked hospital records?"

"Yes, and I didn't find one."

"I can't believe I'm about to say this; the illness seems to be more common in populations of heavily superstitious people. Look for ethnic groups in the area that have a strong belief in werewolves."

"You want me to use ethnic profiling?"

"Sort of. Look, the Irish and the Scottish don't have many werewolf legends. So, lycanthropy is rare in large groups of Scots or Irish. Werewolves are more a Germanic thing, particularly Polish and Czech." I tried not to sigh. "It's also a more common superstition in Native American beliefs. Since you are in Ohio and Indiana, start by asking if anyone has seen Dogmen lately. There are a dozen or so sightings every year. If someone with lycanthropy is running around, the sightings will increase. It's unlikely they will refer to them as a werewolf based on the geographical location. They will call them Dogmen, which is only sort of the same thing, but few people remember the Dogmen myths, just the name."

"I'll start with reports to the police."

"Hey, since you are on here and I'm helping you, you have to help me. Explain why a short serial killer isn't intimidating."

"Like a midget?"

"I don't think that is the politically correct term and no, I don't mean that short. I just mean someone who is petite and below the national average for height."

"Despite being a psychopath, short people are just not intimidating. Fear is a strange thing and we do not usually fear things that are smaller than us."

"What about spiders and snakes?"

"Those are phobias, which as I understand it, is different." Malachi lit a cigarette. The noise of his lighter closing on the other end of the line was loud. "For example, you are intimidating because you rarely hide behind the mask of normality anymore. However, if I was short, because I do appear normal, no one would find me scary. I'm intimidating first because of my physique and second because of my mental condition. You are scary solely for your mental state, and since your surgery, you seem unwilling to put on your mask again, so you are almost always scary."

"How do I explain that to a normal person?"

"You can't. Your mental identification with psychopaths is what keeps you alive. Most people do not have that ability. They consider all people to be relatively the same."

"That is unhelpful."

"Is it a short man or a short woman?"

"Female."

"Then you can't even talk about a Napoleon complex."

"Napoleon was of average height for a man in the 1700's. He did not have a height complex."

"But everyone thinks he did."

"That is actually helpful." I hung up.

The impression of Napoleon is that he was a madman determined to rule the world to make up for being short. However, other world leaders at the time didn't take him seriously, because he was so small. This was not the case. He probably wasn't a madman, just a power obsessed, land-hungry leader, like other leaders at the time. He wasn't short. He wasn't taken as a serious threat because France was pretty bad off after the French Revolution and no one thought he had the money to finance wars. They were wrong.

In my head, a tiny Napoleon was stomping his feet and having a temper tantrum as a much taller James Monroe stared at him. While the image was comical, it cleared my head a little. Short people, even when they were angry, didn't elicit fear from those around them. I drew a stick figure cartoon of the image in my head, clearly labelled the participants, took a picture of it, and sent it to Lucas.

After a few seconds, Lucas responded by telling me to go to bed. A few seconds after that, Xavier texted to see if I was all right. A few more seconds went by before Gabriel sent me a text that said he was laughing out loud. I didn't believe he was. My next text was from Fiona. She had gotten it. It required a woman to understand a woman, even one as dysfunctional as me. She sent a group text explaining the picture. I considered beating my head against the wall.

I was about to put my phone away when it went off again. It was from Nyleena asking me why I was drawing terrible stick figures of Napoleon. I ignored her; it was a conflict of interest.

With Malachi hunting down Dogmen and my phone blissfully not vibrating itself to pieces, I got into bed and turned off the lamp. In the hushed darkness, that stupid voice could talk loud and clear. The one that was convinced our serial killer wasn't just a petite female, but a teenager.

It wasn't the Jiminy Cricket voice that guided my moral decisions. It was my own voice, echoing from the deepest interior of my brain. The voice that had kept me alive over the years. A girl in her late teens would definitely wear that necklace. A girl in high school would love the novelty of it, and since she was smart, she would probably have an idea that the magnetic hematite was considered a healing stone.

I picked up my phone and texted my niece. The text was my email address and a simple sentence: *Need pics of all gold/hematite necklaces you've made.* The necklace wouldn't be one of Cassie's creations, but the pictures would prove exactly how popular the stone was. I hoped her phone was turned off since it was the middle of the night. I didn't need her waking up and flunking a final exam.

At that, my mind did a mental head slap. High stress times were sporadic for teens. For a smart teen looking to get into a good college, exams were definitely high stress times. As were papers, if they still required high school students to write them.

All the pieces fit nicely. A young girl would go with a teen girl, only a few years older than her. A boy would definitely go, and an older teen or twenty-something would not have any concerns about a high school girl giving her a lift. I picked up my phone again, texting Cassie one more time: *What's a booty call?*

Volleyball

The last game of the season was underway.
San Marcos was one point away from winning the
match. The girls moved as a coordinated effort to
keep from losing. If they could win this game, they
would go to the state championship this summer. Jess
really wanted to go to state. It was an honor to be a
captain as a junior. If she could lead her team to
victory here, it would prove that she had not only
deserved it, but had earned it.

Jess backpedaled, reaching for the ball that
had just been served. As it struck her forearms, she
lost her balance. The ball sailed into the air. She
braced for impact with the ground. One of her
teammates jumped, her palm slamming against the
ball, spiking it over the net. Jess slammed into the
floor, arms behind her to catch her.

The ball hit the floor. Game point. The team erupted into celebration. Jess attempted to get up. One arm refused to hold her weight. She fell sideways, impacting with the floor again. Her chin split open. Blood gushed from the wound, falling onto the floor, creating a puddle. The excited shouts died down, replaced by gasps and shrieks.

Jess's forearm was bent at a strange angle. Her hand flopped uselessly. It hurt, but the pain seemed distant and unreal. She stared at it. The gash on her chin completely forgotten.

Her coach ran onto the floor. She was barking instructions, but Jess wasn't sure who they were aimed at. She had never broken a bone before. She'd never even needed stitches. Injuries had always been limited to minor bumps and bruises.

Her mom was suddenly on the floor, next to her. She was talking. The words made no sense. Jess wondered if yellowish marrow was leaking into her body. She wondered if it was mixing with red blood cells to create a thick fluid that would fill her arm. Part of her wanted to see it. The urge to do exactly that was strong. She could push on the broken bone, push it through her skin and watch the marrow leak from it. The thought made her dizzy, not with fear or horror, but excitement and euphoria.

However, no one would understand her desire to see the damage. Gossip would already be spreading about her breaking her arm. Tongues would wag much faster if she were to expose the bone.

A paramedic arrived. Jess stared into her grey eyes. There was no need for a paramedic. Once she was off the floor, she'd be able to walk to the car and go to the hospital. Both her parents were here, one of them could drive her.

The paramedic tilted Jess's head back and began to apply gauze to the chin wound. The paramedic wore purple gloves. Her face was slim, too slim to look healthy. Her eyes had a yellow tinge to them. Jess didn't know what was wrong with the paramedic, but something was. She just didn't look healthy.

Jess debated letting the paramedic touch her. If she was sick, it wasn't unreasonable to think she was contagious. Would that disease infect Jess through the bleeding wound in her chin?

Deciding not to panic her mother any more than necessary, Jess sat still. Her mother was fretting over her arm. Jess realized they had won the game, so they would be going to the state championship. Only, Jess wouldn't be able to play. Her arm would probably be stuck in a cast. She couldn't play volleyball like that.

The tears that began to flow down Jess's face were not from the pain. She could handle that. It was disappointment, disapproval, and frustration. She'd worked really hard to make the team. She'd worked even harder to make sure they won. Now, everyone else would get the credit for her victory.

Some of her teammates could barely tie their shoelaces, let alone organize a winning offense and coordinating an impenetrable defense. Becky probably could, but she was the exception, not the rule. Sure, if they won, Jess's name would be on the winner's plaque. She'd get her picture taken with the trophy, but it wouldn't be the same because she wasn't the winner. That was if they won. Without her, it was very likely her team would lose.

She was loaded into the ambulance and taken to the hospital. The break wasn't as bad as it looked.

She'd only have to wear the cast for six weeks. Six weeks was just long enough for her to miss State. Six weeks would be well into summer. Six weeks would mean writing with her non-dominant hand on her finals. She'd never practiced writing right handed. It would be difficult.

The drive home was filled with sulking and her mother attempting to soothe her hurt feelings. Her mother rehashed all the thoughts Jess had experienced earlier. However, to Jess they were negatives. Her mother seemed to think they were positives.

Jess could see it. The girls on the volleyball court, attempting to man their positions. Her back-up player serving the ball into the net. It would be a disaster. They would leave the state championships with their heads hung low.

There would be no trophy to hoist. No celebrations to partake in. Just a year of hard work and planning to take second place.

Worse, they might not make it out of the preliminary rounds. Second was bad. Anything lower was completely unacceptable. She had not worked this hard to go out in the early rounds. If she could just find a way to delay state championships, life would be better. However, not even death would delay the games. She'd just have to hurry up and heal. There were three weeks until they started. She could be healed in three weeks if she put her mind to it.

Arriving home, Jess went to her room. A plastic bag went around the cast and she got into the bathtub. This was ridiculously difficult. Washing her hair with one hand took an extra-long time. The shampoo had to be squirted directly on her head. Globs of the rosemary and lavender scented soap slipped down her hair and ran down her face before splashing into the water.

She scrubbed as vigorously as possible. Her nails scraped along her scalp, attempting to exfoliate any dead skin in an attempt to keep her dandruff under control. No one knew she had dandruff and that wasn't going to change just because she had broken her stupid arm.

What was wrong with her arm anyway? The fall hadn't been awkward. Her body didn't weigh that much. There was no reason for her arm not to have supported her as she fell.

Her gaze wandered to her cast without her realizing it. They had used hot pink to wrap it. It wasn't her first choice of colors, but they had drugged her for the pain. She hadn't resisted because it would have looked strange if she had. It had been her mother who had suggested the hot pink. She had agreed because of the drugs. Now that they were wearing off, she wasn't entirely happy with the choice.

"Honey, are you okay in there?" Her mother asked, knocking on the door. Her hand stopped scrubbing her head. Her fingers were covered in a pink liquid that ran down her arm. The shampoo was stinging her scalp.

"Fine," she shouted to the closed door.

"Do you need help with your hair or anything?"

"No, I'm good," she submerged her head. The water made her scalp burn even more. It was not entirely unpleasant. She kept her arm above the water as she swished her head back and forth under it. Her head stayed under until she could no longer hold her breath.

The water had a film of strange looking grime on the top of it, the results of using an all-natural shampoo. Artificial lather was omitted from the ingredients, so there weren't any soap bubbles on the surface. The grime was whitish and more distinctive because the water was slightly pink. She'd really have to scrub her fingernails to get all her scalp out from under them.

Standing was tricky. All her weight went on her wet hand and arm. For a moment, she imagined it breaking as well, as if she were suffering from brittle bones or something.

The broken arm kept attempting to help as she dried herself with a towel. It could bend and twist at the elbow, but the wrist and fingers were useless. The cast covered from just below her elbow to just over her first set of knuckles.

She glared at the worthless appendage. It had betrayed her by breaking. She'd fallen on it before playing volleyball and it hadn't broken. The memory of the aluminum bat shaking in her hands came back to her. Was it possible that the bat had injured the bone and the fall had finished it off? It was something she hadn't considered before. Hitting bone was much harder than a baseball. The bat had recoiled with a great deal of force. It seemed at least plausible that there had been an injury at that time.

Getting dressed was frustrating. There was a great deal of wiggling, jumping, and grunting involved. It was harder work than playing volleyball.

Twenty

My email was downloading slowly. It didn't help that I had a principal, my team members, and four other police officers staring at me. Technically, I was waiting for the chief of police. The emails were for another aspect of the case, but since I had time to kill, I had decided it was a good time to download them.

The principal had a stack of papers in front of him. His face told me he was wondering what he was doing with them. It also said he was considering changing his mind. I hoped the chief showed up quickly.

Politicians work on a different schedule than most of us. When he did show up, he had the mayor in tow. I wasn't happy about that, but there was nothing I could do about it.

"Principal Barton, could I please see the enrollment sheets you brought," I asked politely. He slid them to me. I held them up. "Our serial killer is somewhere in this stack of papers. We've been chasing the wrong age group. We thought our killer had to be a college kid either pre-med or med. Last night, I got to thinking about the jewelry that my niece makes. The details are intricate and precise. It doesn't look like a sixteen year old made it. Now, a very smart high school student with an understanding of anatomy and chemistry could in fact make the precision stab wounds that we are looking for. Furthermore, it explains why none of her victims found her threatening. She was their age. Normally, we associate rage with killer teens, but all evidence points to her having Antisocial Personality Disorder with psychopathic tendencies. She wouldn't need to kill because of rage. ASPD psychopaths have extra dopamine receptors and create excessive amounts of norepinephrine and epinephrine. Killing stimulates the excretion of dopamine as well as the two natural types of adrenaline. The bodies have been in clusters, but we've figured out that at least two of the victims in the well and two of the victims in the shed were killed around the same time in late November. If you check school calendars, December is when most teachers schedule mid-terms. Most psychopaths admit that when they are high on adrenaline, they can hyper focus. She's killing when she has exams or papers due because it helps her to focus. Her different disposal methods are being used because she can. She hears about what all these nifty things do in her chemistry classes and she is putting them to good use. Except the shed, which was taken from a TV show or movie, I don't remember which, but I do remember my niece asking me if that was what really happened to people who decomposed in hot, humid climates. She has a car, so she has to be older than sixteen. When you consider two of her victims were younger females, I'm thinking she's closer to sixteen or seventeen."

"While that's an interesting theory, do you have any proof?" The mayor asked. "Last I heard, you needed more than gut feelings to get warrants and arrest people."

"Technically, we don't need evidence," Gabriel reminded him. "However, at this time, we only have the theory. We are not going to start dragging in teens and interrogate them based on a necklace and the fact that our killer is short and female."

"Then we're done," the Chief of Police announced standing up. "This was a mistake."

"The meeting or calling us in?" Gabriel stood up as well. He was taller than the chief was and more intimidating. Not because of his height, but because of his voice and the way he held himself. Gabriel, like Malachi, commanded attention. Gabriel could see a whole pack of wendigos and I would still follow him into the pits of hell to catch the next bad guy.

The chief and mayor said nothing else; they just left. Principal Barton didn't leave. He didn't even stand up. He looked pale.

"You think one of my students is a serial killer?" He asked with a slight quiver in his voice.

"Yes," I answered, "but before you start giving me the names of every juvenile delinquent in attendance, I should point out that our killer will not be a troublemaker. As a matter of fact, if they stick out at all from their peers, it's because of their achievements."

"Do you have any idea how many females in our school are overachievers? We're a satellite city. Most of our students are middle class or better. They vie for positions of academic rank and community service merits. There's greater division between the males, where the world of sports is commended," he told me. "If you were looking for a male, I'd have a list of ten right off the top of my head. But a female, even the bad girls aren't flunking classes."

"Well, we have one piece of evidence that might be helpful," I pulled out the picture of the necklace. Unfortunately, he didn't know who it belonged to. Frustration was starting to set in.

"We do have some artisan jewelry stores. They might be able to help you," the principal said. My frustration decreased a small amount. If it was bought locally we might have an identity for our killer.

"Thank you, that's most helpful," Gabriel said. No one else had bothered to mention the shops. A slip of the mind or lack of understanding to be sure, but that was still irritating. "Aislinn, you're the most knowledgeable; take Lucas."

"Aye, aye," I saluted as I stood up. Lucas and I left the principal behind to deal with the idea that a serial killer was roaming the hallways of his school.

Walking around San Marcos's downtown area was strange. It was a mix of urban and rural lifestyles. Older men in overalls sat on benches, younger women in the latest fashions pushed strollers into small shops. The town wasn't just a satellite for the two major metropolitan areas that existed along the interstate; it was also a community in itself. Farmland touched conservation areas. The city was bustling, but designed as a small town. I was finally beginning to understand it. It wasn't the bedroom communities they talked about on TV; it was a town of blended amenities, catering to both groups of people that called the place home. It was progressive, but wouldn't give up its small town roots.

I could appreciate that. I had grown up in a similar town. Farm boys mixed with the sons of college professors. Stetsons were just as common as Doc Martens. Kids went to the movies as well as hanging out on the backroads.

The first store was a little new age. Crystal pendants hung from the ceiling. The place smelled of patchouli, a special type of hellish incense designed to kill people like me. I tried to hold my breath, but it was hard to talk without breathing.

"Hi, may I help you?" The woman behind the counter was in her fifties. Her smile faltered as she eyed me, within a millisecond it was back. If I hadn't been watching, I might have missed it.

"Hello, US Marshal Aislinn Cain, this is US Marshal Lucas McMichaels," I introduced us as I pulled out my badge and the photo. "We were hoping you knew who made this necklace."

The woman examined the photograph. Glasses materialized out of her shirt. She pulled the picture closer to her face.

"I did," she finally said. "If you look at the clasp, you can just make out my trademark stamp."

"Do you remember who bought it?" I asked.

"It's been a while," the woman pursed her lips together. "I only remember because I thought of how grown up that necklace was for her. She's a high school student here. She comes in with the Mayor's daughter once in a while."

"That is very helpful," I told her, taking back the photo. Lucas said good-bye and we left. Once outside, Lucas glared at me. I stared across the street at a diner. The day's special was pulled pork with French fries. I didn't care about the pulled pork, it was what was under it that caught my attention; extraterrestrial burger with onion rings. I didn't know if that was different from a regular burger, but I did have a weakness for onion rings.

"I feel like we've been transported to New Mexico," Lucas said as he caught sight of the sign.

"UFOs in Texas are rather common. It has one of the highest reported sighting rates of any state; only California has more. The UFO seen in Austin a few nights ago was also seen here and in San Antonio. It makes sense that they would capitalize on it and poke fun at it. I'm just hoping it comes with cheese."

"Are you hungry?"

"We are going to track down the mayor's daughter and find out which of her friends bought the necklace. Food seems like a good idea. I'm thinking we get burgers and take them back to the police station, while Fiona searches for the daughter and then checks her social media to find names of friends."

"Yeah, I am feeling a little peckish myself," Lucas agreed as we crossed the street.

Twenty-One

Fiona's search of Becky Childs' email confirmed that teenagers were idiots. At the very least, they were all miniature sociopaths. Aside from having over a thousand friends listed, the girl, who was sixteen, was a prolific post writer. The girl posted about her meals, her plans to go to the party where Shawn Steiger had gone missing, and there were a ton of pictures of her and another girl. The world didn't need three hundred pictures of Becky Childs and Jessica Blanks. I was informed these were called "selfies."

The better term would have been narcissism. If they had been ancient Greek, some enterprising deity would have turned them into flowers. Nyleena and I had been friends for around twenty years and only had about thirty pictures together.

Becky Childs' entire teenage life was documented by status updates and selfies. If she had a stalker, they would always know where she was, what time she was leaving, what she was doing, and with whom. There was even a selfie, with Shawn and Jess, from the night of the party.

That was particularly interesting. We had been told she wasn't at the party. No one had interviewed Becky Childs or Jessica Blanks. I wondered who had removed their names from the list of guests. It had to be someone within the police department. My money was on the chief of police. It seemed like something he would do. I imagined the mayor and the chief were close.

Gabriel was already on the phone, shouting at someone. I kicked back in my chair and texted Malachi. I had a few minutes while we arranged to meet with Becky and Jessica.

How's the hunt going?

Do you know how many people reported werewolves and Dogmen in the last month? He texted back.

Two. I offered up the random number, knowing that at least one person was crazy in Ohio and Indiana.

Forty-seven!

I had to think about that. That was far more than expected. The suggestion that Malachi go checking on it had been a snipe hunt. I had figured he'd find one or two, go talk to them, find they were batshit crazy and leave me alone while he hunted his phantom werewolf. Finding that forty-seven people had reported seeing one in the past month made me question my tactics. If forty-seven people had reported seeing a werewolf, there might actually be only one crazy person and they were running around in wolf's clothing, literally.

"Forty-seven people have reported seeing a werewolf near the Indiana/Ohio/Michigan border in the last month. Does that seem like an exceptionally high number to anyone else?" I randomly asked.

"Yes," Lucas answered, "especially for a tristate corner. I imagine that's the total number reported in a year in the entire US."

"There are medical conditions that make people very hairy. Perhaps someone with

hypertrichosis is running around, killing people,"
Xavier suggested.

"You'd think with as rare as that is, people
would know if someone in the area had it," Lucas
said. "However, clinical lycanthropy has been known
to make people put on furs when they attack people.
Are the victims being eaten?"

"Eaten? I don't know. I know they are being
bitten and the person doing it has very sharp teeth that
I think are cosmetic."

"That rules out clinical lycanthropy. Someone
with those sorts of delusions would not plan such a
physical alteration, because they would believe it
would happen naturally. It sounds like he has a crazy
guy running around the woods, wearing a fur coat and
fake teeth, because he likes chewing on people,"
Lucas told me.

"You should tell him that," I told Lucas.

"Sure," Lucas hit a few buttons on his phone
and began texting. He had some fancy smart phone
that was more complicated than my iPhone. I had
attempted to use it a few times, but had given up
because it sucked. Or I did, I wasn't sure which.

"Well, the Mayor is stonewalling," Gabriel said.

"Fine with me, I don't mind putting my shoulder to his door," Lucas answered.

"There is nothing worse than a pompous ass who thinks that just because he's a politician, he's above the law," Xavier added. "The mayor of San Marcos seems just such a man."

"Those types of men tend to be verbally abusive to underlings and children. Wonder how he feels about his daughter?" Lucas commented. "Especially since she seems to be attracted to guys without a brain. Judging by her photos, she has a thing for that kid, Matt Dover. I had the pleasure of interviewing him, it's a good thing he has money and a pretty face, because he isn't going far on his brain power."

"His buddy, Simon Westbrook, has the same problem. I keep wondering if Cassie's life is this dramatic. Surely it isn't, she's a smart girl," I said.

"It is," Lucas informed me. "Teen girls, and boys for that matter, lead dramatic lives because they are all mentally underdeveloped. This makes just about everything a crisis. When everything is a crisis, life is dramatic."

"I don't remember this sort of drama in my teen years."

"You are asexual and were extremely mature for your age. There was no need for your life to be in constant crisis and, therefore, it was less dramatic," Lucas told me.

"Let's go," Gabriel started out the door. I didn't know if we were headed to William Childs' house to interview his daughter or the Blanks' house to interview their daughter. For the most part, I didn't care. I was ready to do some hard-core interrogating and if I got to bust down a door or Taser someone, well that was a bonus.

The house was a nice two story, with blue vinyl siding and a large window on the front door. These doors were incredibly unsafe and I wouldn't have owned one if my life depended on it. Of course, there were times when my life probably had depended upon it, which proved my point.

A middle-aged woman with blond hair and blue eyes answered the door. She smiled at us, but it didn't look real. Her make-up was light and perfectly understated.

"Mrs. Blanks?" Gabriel asked.

"Yes," she answered.

"US Marshal Gabriel Henders; this is the SCTU team. Is your daughter, Jessica, friends with Shawn Steiger and Becky Childs?"

"Yes," she answered.

"Have you been made aware that we found Shawn deceased yesterday?"

"No, I hadn't been," she paused. "Oh, that's why, yes, I see now. Um, what can I do for you?"

"We'd like to talk to you and Jessica if possible. We just discovered that she was at a party Saturday. That was the last time that Shawn was seen alive. We've interviewed everyone except her and Becky Childs," Gabriel informed her.

"Of course, come in." Mrs. Blanks held open the door. "I'm not sure how much help Jess will be though. She had a volleyball game this afternoon and broke her arm. They have her pretty heavily medicated."

"It won't take long," Lucas reassured her. Her shoulders relaxed, her face changed a little. Despite being the size of a very large ogre, Lucas had that effect on people.

Normally, we didn't use three people to do an interview, but this was a special case. Since all teens did indeed exhibit symptoms of sociopathology, Lucas and Gabriel couldn't always figure out if they were just being teens or if they were really on the downhill side of becoming the next Ted Bundy. Xavier stayed by the car. I sat down in an uncomfortable chair while Mrs. Blanks called to Jessica. Lucas and Xavier sat on the couch. There was only one seat left, so I stood. I wanted Jessica and Mrs. Blanks to sit; they would be at the disadvantage if they were seated.

"Jessie, this is US Marshal Gabriel Henders and he wants to talk to you about the party on Saturday. I'm sorry; I didn't catch the rest of your names."

"Sorry; US Marshal Lucas McMichaels and US Marshal Aislinn Cain," Gabriel introduced us. I didn't smile, it would have been upsetting.

"Jessica," Lucas began, "do you remember seeing Shawn on Saturday night?"

"Yeah, of course," Jessica Blanks sat in the chair I had vacated. "Everyone calls me Jess or Jessie though. Is Shawn all right?"

"I'm afraid not. We found him yesterday."

"He was murdered?" Jessica asked.

"We're not sure yet," Lucas lied through his teeth. Her voice caught my attention, there was a tone to it, something that wasn't right in the way she posed the question. The sun was setting on Texas and Xavier's form was starting to blend into the surrounding area. My teeth grated as my other two teammates asked Jessica questions. Finally, I pulled the picture of the necklace from my jacket.

"Are you familiar with this piece of jewelry?" I asked her.

"Yes, I bought it a while ago, for a friend." She made no expression.

"Does your friend have a name?" I asked.

"Esperanza Pena," Jessica answered. She still hadn't mentioned that Esperanza was missing. This struck me as odd. You'd think a teenager with one friend dead and another missing would have something to say. So far, the only name released was Nathan's. We'd kept the other identities secret.

"Why did you buy it for her?" I continued.

"Because it was her birthday and she liked things like that."

"I see," I answered. "When did you give it to her?"

"On her birthday. She had a really bad day, her house was robbed, and then her car broke down, so I drove to meet her. We had dinner together, I left her at the electronics store because she said she'd call someone to come get her and I had to get home from San Antonio on a weeknight. No one's seen her since."

"You didn't tell me that," Mrs. Blanks interjected. "Why didn't you tell me you knew the missing girls from San Antonio?"

"I don't know them all, I just know Esperanza; she played volleyball." Jessica snapped at her mother.

Twenty-Two

Sleeping had been fitful. Malachi had texted several times. My waking mind wanted to dwell on our serial killer and how she got around as she did.

The problem with psychopaths was that they were psychopaths. Even the ones who weren't out chopping people up, weren't exactly "good people." They were very adept at making it look like their hearts were in the right place, but in reality, everything they did benefited themselves. Malachi for example, even when he was looking out for me, it was being done because looking out for me was in his best interest.

Jessica Blanks was a sixteen-year-old psychopath with a high IQ and social skills. She was also very dangerous. Psychopaths tended to live in their own versions of reality. They had very rich fantasy lives and when the real thing failed to meet up to the standards of the fantasy world, they became moody.

Sociopaths and psychopaths had pulled the greatest trick in the history of mankind. Malachi and I both knew it, but we didn't discuss it. My brain tumor had revealed the secret to some degree, but no one had caught on, because they bought the lie.

I hadn't suddenly learned to feel because I had a tumor in my head. I hadn't been able to turn it off because of the tumor. Our emotions worked on switches, so to speak. They could be turned on or off. For most of us, it was easier to turn them off and keep them there. When they were on, we tended to become violent, sadistic, rage-filled monsters.

There were triggers for those switches as well. Mine was the intimate group of people that I considered my equals, my mother, Nyleena, my team, Malachi, and to some degree, my sister-in-law and her children. I was Malachi's biggest weakness, but he had a few others. In moments of hedonistic sadism, we liked to push each other's buttons and see just how angry the other person could get.

We could even empathize when forced into the right situation. If someone were torturing Nyleena, I would be able to empathize with her. Her pain would become mine. It was why I would go to great lengths to kill who ever hurt her. They would be hurting me as well. We were every bit as narcissistic as we claimed. Our reality revolved around us.

Aside from a few neurological changes that caused psychopaths not to feel pain or understand fear, the greatest difference between a sociopath and a psychopath was the length of time they held onto those emotions. Psychopaths held on longer, it was the reason their rage was stronger.

It was why we were drawn to one another like a compass finding magnetic north. It was easy for a sociopath or psychopath to find a kindred spirit. We knew exactly what to look for; we knew all those dirty little secrets that we kept hidden from mankind. We sought each other out because we could derive the greatest pleasure from forcing another of our sort to feel.

It made us vulnerable. Once I had realized that Jessica's tears were only half-real and her soft tone carried hints of anger, I had instantly found her Achilles' heel. Becky Childs sat in a conference room with Lucas and her father, the mayor. Becky was as crucial to Jessica as Nyleena was to me. Even a soft interrogation, which is what she was currently enduring, would be gut wrenching for Jessica.

At the moment, I felt nothing for the upset sixteen year old in the other room. My emotions had been off as much as possible since the tumor had been removed. Feeling wasn't just exhausting, it made me angry. I wasn't even bothering with the fake half-emotions that I used to mask my condition. Even those pissed me off.

Becky's tears, which were very real, only made me sigh with irritation. Lucas was carefully bullying her, trying to get some sort of statement about Jessica being off. We didn't need much evidence that Jessica was our serial killer, but my gut reaction to her being a psychopath wasn't going to do it this time. Lucas had picked up on hints of it, but to him, they could have also just been teenage angst. No one but me was willing to throw the captain of the volleyball team and valedictorian candidate into The Fortress based on a necklace.

"Cain," Gabriel whispered my name and touched my shoulder. He was standing. I could have sworn he was sitting a few moments ago.

"What?" I whispered back.

"They found a body they want us to look at. Lucas is busy, so you'll have to help Xavier."

"I usually do," I reminded him.

"I meant with the psychobabble," Gabriel corrected himself.

"I'm not a psychologist."

"You're the closest I've got that isn't busy. Go with Xavier. Call me when you come to some conclusions." He motioned for me to leave.

I did as I was told. He wasn't going to let me go in there with a phone book anyway. It would be better for me not to watch the interrogation of Becky Childs.

It was dark. Xavier kept throwing glances my way though. The shadows in the car would change when he did it. I stared out the front window, not wanting to deal with whatever was on his mind.

He stopped the SUV in front of a house with a squad car already there. The house looked older than the pyramids and in worse condition. The lights from the car were violently bright. The strobe burned my eyes and made them water. I held my hand up to my forehead to block as much of it as possible. Xavier was walking towards a barn.

The barn was in good condition. Was it a Texas thing to let the house go to ruin, but keep the barn looking nice? I didn't know and I didn't figure asking was going to win me many points, points that I might need in the future. After all, I was an interloper and no one really liked interlopers.

The air in the barn was fresh. Both large doors stood open. Aside from the smell of grass and hay, I caught a hint of freshly smoked pot and below that, decomposition. I put balm under my nose as I caught sight of Nails, the Doberman. He wagged his tail as he sat on the hard floor.

"What's with the dog?" Xavier asked.

"The boys that found the bodies panicked and couldn't remember how they got to it." Young appeared out of a hole. "So they called me to come relocate the entrance. I'll admit it was well hidden, but their condition might have hampered their memories."

"I take it that the smell is their pot," I said.

"I can't believe you can still smell it," Young said. "That was two hours ago."

"It lingers," I shrugged. "Our serial killer?"

"It doesn't look like it," Young told me, "but I'm not an expert."

Xavier went down the strangely built steps first. They terminated about six feet underground. Xavier was standing up, but only just. I had no trouble standing in the root cellar, but it felt cramped.

The smell was also worse. The bodies were fresh. Scavengers had gotten to them, most likely rats and mice, but possibly a few burrowing animals. Xavier's flashlight caught bone in the corner. We both walked towards it.

One body was a few days older than the other, based on how they looked. The newest one had only been down here a day, maybe two. It was still bloated. Black ooze dripped out of the nose when Xavier rolled it over.

They were nothing like our other kills. These had not died quickly from a stab wound to the heart. They had been beaten. Bones jutted out at odd angles. A quick look told me one of them was Sabrina Reeves, a teen that had gone missing last week. The other was unidentified, even though it was the newcomer to the pit.

While Sabrina's body had been battered, it looked practically peaceful compared to the other. Only one of Sabrina's legs was broken. The other suffered two shattered legs, including a broken femur that poked through the flesh of the thigh.

Cloudy blue eyes caught my attention. I leaned in closer to the body. My memory wasn't as good as Malachi's, but it was good and I had seen those eyes before. Slowly, my brain began reconstructing the face. The jaw and cheekbones had been crushed. Skin had been split open and ripped off. The nose was nearly gone, most likely broken by the attacker and then eaten by rodents.

"Simon Westbrook," I told Xavier.

"I'll be damned, I think you're right," Xavier answered. "He really pissed someone off. This is a lot of rage. A whole lot of rage, not just overkill for fun and enjoyment. I can't even begin to think of what kind of weapon the assailant used."

"Me either," I was pulling out my phone.

Ask Becky if Jessica Blanks had a thing for Simon Westbrook. I texted Gabriel.

Is that the victim? He asked.

No, that's one of the victims. I answered. We have two. Ask about Sabrina Reeves too.

Jesus Christ. I put the phone away, recognizing that as the end of the conversation for now.

"I think she hobbled him," Xavier said to me. He was pointing at Simon's knees. They were both dislocated. "I'm guessing those were done upstairs, then she shoved him down here and continued the assault. When he died, she just kept hitting him."

"She?" I asked.

"A guy isn't standing up down here and getting a swing going, so yeah, she. Despite the brutality, I would say it's the same killer. These were more personal though. She beat the shit out of both of them."

"Hammer? Crowbar? Baseball bat?" I asked.

"For Sabrina Reeves, maybe a baseball bat. There's some dark bruises on her arms and back that would be the right width. For Simon, it was smaller than a baseball bat, but it might have been harder. The wounds are worse."

"Smaller because she could only use one arm," I pointed out.

"Maybe or maybe because she really hated him, more than Sabrina." Xavier stepped back from the bodies. "I know what made Simon's injuries."

"That was fast."

"I've seen it before. She must have been furious."

"Well don't keep me in the dark, literally and figuratively," I snipped.

"You have too, just not this particular kind," he pulled a small object off my hip. With a flick of his wrist and push of a button, my carbon steel expandable baton became a menacing piece of equipment. "She used a baton, but not one meant for self-defense. It's a Mace Baton. They have full metal cores, instead of rubber."

Twenty-Three

It turned out that Mace Batons were used mostly for military ceremonies. Jessica's brother was a military graduate. Becky confirmed that Jessica had a crush on Simon Westbrook. She also told us that a few weeks ago, Sabrina Reeves and Simon Westbrook had been caught making out in a bathroom at school. Sabrina had been suspended. Simon had gotten detention. The world was an unjust place.

It was about to get a lot more unjust. I knew because I was standing outside Jessica Blanks' house in the middle of the night with a warrant we didn't need. Her best friend was still at the police station, under lock and key, so that she couldn't warn Jessica that we were asking questions about the girl.

The lyrics to *Angry Johnny* by Poe was playing in my head. It seemed appropriate since it was about a girl wanting to kill a guy. Of course, in the song, the girl seems to be doing it for revenge, since she claims she's in Hell. Jessica had just been pissed because Simon didn't seem interested in her.

The house was quiet. The lights were all off. There had been some debate about breaking down the door and ringing the doorbell. I had eventually lost and Gabriel rang the doorbell.

Upstairs, lights began popping on. The sound of feet could be heard. Gabriel hammered his fist against the wooden frame of the front door.

Mr. Blanks opened the door. His eyes were wild, his face confused and terrified. He really had no idea why we were beating on his door in the middle of the night. Ironically, at this exact moment, a much nicer person was knocking on the door of the Westbrook's house to tell them their son was dead.

"Mr. Blanks, we need to see your daughter, immediately," Gabriel's voice was stern.

"What is this about?" Mr. Blanks acted like any other father on the planet when people were demanding to see his daughter in the middle of the night.

"What is it, Richard?" Mrs. Blanks asked on the verge of panic.

"US Marshals Serial Crimes Tracking Unit," Gabriel pushed his way in the front door. Lucas went in behind him. "Where is Jessica Blanks?" Gabriel demanded again. I stepped off the porch. If Jessica wasn't responding to our midnight visit, she was either drugged out of her mind or she was about to do something really stupid.

A shadow flashed by the corner of my eye. She had chosen wrong.

"We've got a runner," I shouted, taking off after the shadow. The girl was faster than I was, lighter than me, but she hadn't been crazy as long as I had. I used that to my advantage.

The irritation slipped away from me. I let the darkness sweep through me. Being completely empty is hard to describe, but in that void, the restraints my mind put on my body lifted. My pace picked up just a touch, my stride lengthening as it did. My heart rate slowed, despite the increased cardio. The muscles in my legs would tear themselves in pieces before they tired and gave out on me. My heart would explode in my chest before it stopped pumping oxygenated blood through my system. Here, I felt no pain and with it, no restrictions.

The shadow turned a corner a dozen feet ahead of me. My brain didn't think. I overran the corner, entering the street before I turned. Instincts trying to keep me from being ambushed. There wasn't an ambush, the shadow was moving down the street, away from me.

I was closing the distance. The shadow knew it. Her breathing was starting to become ragged. Her body suffocating under the strain of her sprint. It was slowing down without her approval. I slowed down as I neared.

When she turned on me, her face was contorted. Rage oozed from her. Spittle dripped from her lips and her eyes were wild, showing too much white. She came at me, arms extended. Her hand clawed at me, trying to grab my hair. She raised her cast, bringing it down on my shoulder.

My hand did find flesh. The fingers dug into the nape of her neck. I drew back to punch her in the face and found myself staring into the face of a sixteen year old. She was a killer, but she was also a teen. Some part of me knew that and my arm relaxed, grabbing her instead. I spun her up, cocooning her into me, like a mother cradling an unruly two year old. She twisted and screamed. I kept my arms around her, kept her arms pinned to her chest. I squeezed tighter, fitting her smaller body into mine, using my height and weight advantage to keep her secure.

She kicked me. The rubber sole tore hide from my leg. I put more weight on her, forcing her down. We both ended up on our knees. I leaned into her.

"You might be good at killing your classmates, but you've never come across someone like me. So, settle down and wait," I whispered to her. Her body relaxed, leaning into me. We waited, quietly.

The sound of a car starting drifted on the night air. Lights were coming on in the houses around us. Someone shouted to call the police. I didn't announce that I was the police. My attention couldn't be divided. No matter how much my brain said she was sixteen, my instincts knew she was a psychopath.

She started to squirm a little. I pulled her into me, tighter, forcing her to breathe hard as her lungs failed to inflate fully.

"Hey, get off her!" Some man shouted at me.

"US Marshals!" I shouted back at him. He held up a flashlight. It bounced off my shiny badge attached to my jacket. She squirmed again, her arm breaking free. I reached for it, pushing us both forward into the pavement. She grunted as my weight landed on top of her and her broken arm. There should have been more noise. She should have screamed. I moved fast, pulling my handcuffs. The man took another step towards us. The sound of metal hitting concrete seemed very loud in the darkness. He screamed.

She rolled, catching my hip with her cast, trying to shove me off. I repositioned, straddling her hip. The blade was cold as it slid into my side. I didn't grab at it; instead, I grabbed her wrist. There was a moment of surprise on her face. She had expected me to look and sound like all her victims. I didn't. She really hadn't met another person so much like herself. She began struggling again.

The man was still screaming. He had fallen to the ground. I wanted to tell him to shut up and suck it up, it was just a foot, but I didn't. The cast slipped from Jessica's wrist as she pulled out from under me. The girl was on her feet in almost no time. She kicked me, landing a blow on my jaw. My tongue started to bleed, filling my mouth. I spit it out as I rocked backwards and up onto my feet.

Sixteen or not, I reached for my baton. It wasn't there. My eyes locked on hers as the distinct click came to my ears. That's what she had been doing on my hip. I hated fighting psychopaths; they were relentless.

"Don't do it, Jessica," I warned. "I will Taser you."

Jessica didn't seem impressed by the threat. She took a step towards me. My hand found the Taser, pulled it from its holster and fired. She took another step. I ejected the cartridge, turning it into a stun gun. The cartridge was blue as it clattered to the ground. My cartridges were not blue, they were orange. I was fairly certain that when I survived this, I was going to have to kill Fiona on principle.

The baton hit my arm. My elbow hit the handle of the knife, burying it even deeper into my side. The elbow dislocated from the double impact. She swung it again. It made a noise similar to a whip as swung through the air. I turned just enough to keep the blow from hitting my hip. It slammed into my buttocks instead. The skin split, soaking my jeans instantly. I caught the tip of the baton and jerked. She stumbled into me. I elbowed her in the chest, using her own momentum to knock the wind out of her.

"Shoot her!" Someone shouted. I turned to see who was shouting and at who. The baton slipped from my fingers. I didn't draw my guns. I drew a knife. The baton landed a brutal blow to my shoulder. Bone shuddered under it. I turned into it, taking the full impact with the bad arm. My knife slipped into her flesh. She looked shocked. She stumbled back from me. I rushed her, taking us both to the ground. The baton landed another, weaker blow. My head started bleeding. The world went out of focus. I struggled to find my footing and vomited instead.

The shadows of people came into view. I vomited again. I let myself fall over sideways. The knife hilt pierced my skin as it connected with the concrete. I closed my eyes to stop the world from spinning. Blood ran down my head, mixing with my hair before landing on the pavement. I wasn't sure if she had hit my head or my ear. It didn't matter. She had rocked my world with that hit. I had vertigo.

"Jesus Christ," Xavier's voice came to me.

"Get her, I'm fine."

"You are not fine." Xavier informed me.

"She's a killer. Get her," I barked.

"She's wounded and leaving a blood trail. Someone else can get her. I'm going to deal with you. Now shut up and let me look you over."

"If you open my eyelids and shine any lights into my eyes, I'll stab you." I had already pulled a knife.

"That's new," Xavier's hands touched my forehead. "You aren't cold. How much pain are you in?"

"I just got my ass kicked by a sixteen year old. I'm not in pain. I'm really, really angry."

"And bleeding from multiple places. Five that I can see. I'm worried about your head. Did she hit the back?"

"I don't know."

"Can you roll up and let me look?"

"If a chunk of my skull has fallen out, do you really want to expose my brain to onlookers?"

"If a chunk of your skull fell out, that is the least of my concerns." He rolled me onto my side. I vomited again. He swore, so I was guessing it hit him. "She damn near tore your ear off and ruptured your ear drum, which is causing the vertigo. You'll need to be checked for a concussion. Aside from the knife, what weapons did she have?"

"Little bitch made off with my baton."

"That would definitely do this kind of damage. Your ass is bleeding."

"That will need stitches. And I'm getting back that baton."

"Oh, I have no doubt."

Twenty-Four

My body felt heavy. My brain felt foggy, and even though I wasn't completely awake, I knew I was having a bad day. I could smell antiseptic. Either I was in a morgue or in a recovery room. Considering my brain was attempting to work, I guessed it was a recovery room. Prying apart my eyelids took an act of God, signed in triplicate, and delivered by snail. At first, my vision was blurry, but a shadow sat near me.

"Well, I'm not dead, but I am exceptionally thirsty," I told the shadow.

"I'll get you some water and let the doctor know you're awake," a female voice answered. It wasn't Fiona, so I didn't start looking for ways to kill her. My brain instantly caught up. I had passed out, bleeding on the road, after getting my ass handed to me by a sixteen-year-old psychopath who had used my own baton to do it. I'd also been stabbed, in the side, there was a good chance that I had lost a kidney.

"Marshal Cain," a small, round man with no hair and a wide smile walked into the room. He didn't have the accent I expected. "We had to repair your colon and part of your small intestine, clean everything out well, and remove an ovary."

"What's the bad news?" I asked.

"Most women think the removal of an ovary is a bad thing," he said to me, looking down at my chart.

"Better than a kidney."

"Well, when you look at it that way. The knife went in at an angle, which is what saved you. It only nicked your colon and small intestine. The hilt entering the wound caused some internal bruising. If the knife had been an inch or two longer, you would have lost your uterus."

"Great, when do I get out of here?" I asked.

"A few days. The first day is the most critical. You'll need help getting up and down. You are going to be extremely sore. Do you remember the incident?"

"How many stitches to my butt? How's my ear?"

"We reattached your ear, your eardrum is ruptured, so don't go swimming any time soon. Part of the top cartilage was removed, but a plastic surgeon might be able to do something, if you want. As for your rear end, that was actually the worst injury, as far as scarring. I understand you were struck with an extendable baton and it left a mark very similar to a whip. It required over a hundred stitches to close. You're going to have to take it easy, we couldn't put in staples and stitches rip out easier."

I frowned. Hospitals were hard on normal people. On someone like me, they were pure torture. There was nothing to do. The drugs made you feel like crap. They lowered your ability to focus on anything and I needed something to focus on or I would go out of my mind. My heartbeat picked up just a little. My blood pressure increased. I watched the monitors, watched my body going into sensory deprivation mode. I needed something to focus my mind on.

The light outside my window caught my attention. I stared at it, as if it could rescue me from the dungeon that was my own mind. As I stared, I realized that there were three days until the full moon. I hit the button on my bed, calling for the nurse.

"I need my phone. I need to call someone," I told her.

"You can't have a phone until morning, Marshal Cain," she responded.

"It's important!" I pleaded.

"No." She turned to walk away.

"Fine, contact the FBI office in San Antonio, tell them to have Malachi Blake contact you," I scribbled the note for Malachi down on a piece of paper and handed it to her. Her face contracted and paled. The note wasn't that bad. However, I might as well have handed her a ticking bomb.

"I'll get your phone," she told me, crumbling up the note.

"Aren't you supposed to be recovering?" Malachi's voice didn't sound as if he'd been sleeping, but that didn't mean much with Malachi.

"You've got a full moon coming," I told him.

"So?"

"So, if your killer is pretending to be a werewolf, he'll be all decked out in his strange skins when the moon finally enters that phase. You can catch him by following the number of wolf and werewolf calls that night."

"That may be a problem," Malachi told me.
"Why?"

"I've been reassigned, temporarily. You will be too, tomorrow, or the next day." Malachi hung up. We were both about to be reassigned. That couldn't be good. Had someone broken out of the Fortress? My mind instantly conjured up images of Patterson and Eric running free in their grey jumpsuits. Grey was supposed to be soothing. I wasn't sure if it was or not. I didn't find it soothing, I found it irritating, but I wasn't a normal person. Of course, neither were Patterson and Eric, so maybe they didn't find grey soothing either.

There was no TV remote. If I was being temporarily reassigned, it meant that Jessica Blanks wasn't in custody yet. It also meant the evil teenager still had my baton. I wasn't sure which of those pissed me off more. They were equally annoying. I should have had her. There was no way she should have been able to get my baton.

Yet she had. Because she was sixteen. My humanity had leaked through. I had let a sixteen-year-old get the better of me because I hadn't wanted to kill her. I hadn't wanted to beat her to a pulp with the harsh, carbon steel baton. I'd attempted non-lethal control while dealing with a psychopath and I was paying the price.

It wasn't the stitches or the knife wound or the fact that I was now in a hospital. My punishment was knowing that I had ignored my own rule. When dealing with a psychopath, lethal violence was the norm, not the exception. I could and should have shot her. I should have broken out the baton and beat her into submission. I should have had control of the situation from beginning to end.

However, because she was sixteen, I had never been in control. Sociopath or psychopath, she had reminded me of my niece and I had ended up getting the shit beat out of me because of it. Her age had quieted the monster that lurked in the silent darkness within my soul. I was lucky the little bitch hadn't killed me.

Then there was the Taser. That stupid blue cartridge that had ejected from it, after firing, had also been working against me. It hadn't had the charge to drop the psychopathic teenager. It had simply pissed her off. I knew because they pissed me off when I got hit by them. There was no doubt that was Fiona's doing, and I was just starting to like her. Now, I wanted to pop in an orange cartridge and use it on her. Of course, it would probably kill her, but I was okay with that. She had nearly gotten me killed by replacing the cartridge with a lower output model.

Yet, she had been blinded by the same thing I had. The age of our killer. It was one thing to chase adults who killed. It really was different when the killer was practically a child. The part of me with a history degree reminded me that sixteen wasn't really young, definitely not child-like. However, the part of me that dealt with serial killers on a regular basis disagreed. Sixteen was definitely old enough to be a killer. Sixteen was definitely old enough to be tried as an adult and sent to The Fortress. Even sixteen year olds had the impulse to kill, and not enough maturity to control it.

Maybe it wasn't entirely Fiona's fault. Even without the Taser, I could have subdued her. I could have broken her other arm. I could have strangled her until she passed out. I could have overpowered her. I didn't.

Now, I was beating myself up over it in the hospital. We should have been on a plane, heading home or to wherever this big secret thing Malachi was working on existed.

This was why sociopaths shouldn't have time to themselves. At least not much of it. Aside from building up our own egos and self-aggrandizing, we could be rather brutal, and it gave us time to place blame. My heartbeat sped up a little more. My blood pressure ticked up another couple of notches. My anger was beginning to seep out of the place where I tried to keep it contained.

I hit the button on the Demerol. The liquid was suddenly coursing through my veins. The drug helped, but my mind continued to spiral. My anger continued to grow. I studied the machine. It wanted a code to access it. The nurses had typed in a code earlier, when they had set it up. I had been half-asleep. It was seven digits long. My brain searched for the memory. Once found, the movement of her fingers gave me the knowledge I desired.

I punched in the code. It unlocked, giving me access to the dosage. I considered my current state. Valium or Ativan would have been better, but I wasn't on either of those. Demerol was all they were giving me except saline and antibiotics. I didn't need a super dose of either of those. I needed something to help me control my anger. Demerol could do it, if it could force me to sleep. However, in small doses, Demerol didn't work like that, not on me. It wasn't strong enough to dull my mind and my mind did a better job of controlling the pain.

Remembering Xavier's lecture on Demerol, I selected a dosage and typed it in. The plunger on the automated machine depressed. The second, larger dose hit my veins. Coursing through me, it began to have the desired effect on my brain. A fog began to settle on it. The anger, which was threatening to overtake me, subsided, unable to continue to flame and explode because the fuel source had been shut down. My senses dulled.

My nose, which had been smelling antiseptic and a sickly sweet odor associated with illness, stopped working. For a moment, I wondered if this was how Malachi smelled the world. His olfactory system was underdeveloped. His sense of smell was terrible and his sense of taste was altered by it.

Then the world began to darken. Tunnel vision and dancing flashes of light filled my eyes. The lids closed against the spectacle, but even closed, I could still feel them. This was exactly what I needed. I'd shot up enough Demerol to trigger a migraine.

The pain exploded in my head. The world fell away. There was only the pain.

Twenty-Five

"Were you trying to kill yourself?" Gabriel shouted.

"No, she was trying to induce a migraine," Xavier's voice was much quieter. "She does that from time to time. It stops whatever is about to happen to her."

"Like…" Gabriel didn't finish. He flopped into a chair and sighed. It was hard being my boss. I knew it.

"I should not be left to rot in a hospital with nothing but my own mind for entertainment." I held up my phone, which was very dead. It had died during my reconfiguring of the Demerol dosage. The dosage needed for the migraine had actually been an overdose. I hadn't thought of it when I did it. I had just known that I needed something to control my rage. Migraines were the ultimate control.

The door to my room was shut. Lucas was taking up one chair. Xavier was futzing with the machine. Gabriel was sitting in the other chair.

"Why is the door shut?" I asked.

"We can't have the hospital staff hearing Gabriel chew you out for the overdose. They think something went wrong with the machine," Lucas informed me. "Were you trying to kill yourself?"

"No." I answered. "Look, I know it's unconventional, but you have never been locked in my brain. If I didn't stop thinking, I was going to start doing something worse. So, I programmed the machine to give me a small overdose. Demerol can trigger migraines. As violent as I get when I have them, I don't normally start killing people. I had to shut my brain down. The Demerol induced migraine did exactly that."

"And made you sleep for nearly thirty hours," Xavier said. "She's right. The dosage she gave herself was only an overdose because of the amount she had injected using the button immediately before it."

"Next time, fake a panic attack," Gabriel told me. "How do you feel?"

"Honestly, really good. I always get the best sleep on large doses of drugs," I admitted. "I had no dreams, nothing bothered me. It was nice, really restful. The medically induced coma was not as restful. How's the manhunt?"

"Hindered," Gabriel sighed. "You have less than twelve hours of bedrest left. Soon, you and Xavier are going to be requested in Houston, by the CDC. Malachi is already there."

"Xavier and I?" I looked at him.

"It seems that as an undergrad, you wrote a paper on how bubonic plague spread so easily through Constantinople during the reign of Justinian, and then equated that with modern day cities. They would like you to consult."

"Modern day cities would be excellent places to release bubonic plague, if you wanted maximum casualties," I told him.

"Don't go into the specifics." Gabriel held up his hand. "I read your paper, as did Xavier and just about every epidemiologist in the country. Houston has had ten people diagnosed with bubonic plague in the last twenty-four hours. It's the strain they saw in California last year and it is antibiotic resistant. Since the strain was engineered in a lab and stolen, they are considering this dissemination as intentional. You are the expert that will accompany the VCU to find the person responsible."

"I do not like working with Malachi," I told Gabriel.

"We will be joining as soon as we find Jessica Blanks. Everyone is trying to keep this quiet to stop the crisis that will happen when the information gets leaked out. Nothing like bringing back the Black Death to start chaos and panic," Lucas told me.

"Uh, yeah, what if I don't want to go?" I asked.

"Why wouldn't you want to go?" Gabriel asked.

"Someone sent me a dead squirrel with that particular strain of plague. My guess is it's the same someone that has managed to infect people in Houston. Only, here's the problem, humans are a terrible host for plague. So, how the hell are they disseminating it? They aren't injecting the people directly. Most mammals die within a few days of infection. That makes this particular killer the craziest person to ever live. Because they have spent time breeding rats to carry the fleas and then released the damn rats into the city to infect other animals, which is why it is now infecting humans. In my paper, rats passed it to pets, pets passed it to owners in the form of fleabites. Problem is, we've invented the vacuum cleaner and that is the leading cause of flea death in the world. This isn't some third world country where diseases spread from poor hygiene. This has been well thought out, well planned, and well executed. If it is not a scientist, it is someone that was going to be a scientist. The problem with lab rats is they die at the end, and anyone going into Houston is a lab rat. We'd be better off to nuke the city."

"I don't think dropping nuclear bombs on Houston is an acceptable option," Xavier giggled. "Besides, cockroaches survive."

"But fleas do not," I sighed. "In reality, my paper was written to get me an A. It isn't feasible, not really, because we've done what we can to eliminate fleas."

"Ten people would disagree with you," Malachi walked into the room. "I'm here to escort you, if you are well enough."

"I'm not. I have a ruptured ear drum, stitches in my behind, and a stab wound that took out an ovary."

"That was two days ago," Malachi said.

"It's a lot of trauma to recover from."

"Are you concerned about getting the plague?" Xavier asked.

"Slightly," I admitted. "If it was just bubonic plague, that would be one thing, but it isn't, it is antibiotic resistant bubonic plague. It's a nightmare situation. It's also the sort of thing that caused millions to die in the fourteenth century. Plague only becomes super deadly once in a while."

"I'm aware, I am a doctor," Xavier reminded me.

"Well, this is one of those times."

"We have HAZMAT suits," Malachi joined in. "Let these guys catch your serial killer, we'll go get the bastard that has released plague into the Lone Star State."

"Bitch, actually," Lucas said from his seat. "You're most likely looking for a woman. This is essentially the same as poisoning, plus it took nurturing to breed the rats and this particular strain of bubonic plague for years. If I remember right, it was stolen a while ago from a lab at a campus. While a man would release a virus or bacteria to kill, it'd be anthrax or something similar. It would not have been something that needed nurturing like a child."

"Oh goody, I can get my ass kicked by another girl," I snipped. "Everyone out, I have to put clothing on."

"Um, no," Lucas informed me. "Everyone but me needs to leave. You are going to need help with clothing."

"I'm fine."

"You're not fine and if your government wasn't in the middle of a meltdown, you wouldn't be going," he told me. I smiled. At least someone cared about it. The smile faded. I was feeling sorry for myself. It wasn't a pleasant emotion. I didn't need pity parades with ticker tape and confetti, especially not ones thrown by me. It was my fault, all of it, and I knew it; hence the pity parade. I could point fingers at anyone I wanted, but the truth was I had not treated her like a psychopath, I had treated her like I would have wanted someone to treat my niece. I might as well have used the baton on myself.

This wasn't new information. It wasn't earth-shattering revelations. It was the stuff I had been hiding from for the last thirty odd hours. Admitting my failures didn't make me feel better about myself, it made me angry. I didn't need reminders that I could be human, if I decided to be. I needed a reminder of the monster that shared this fragile human shell. I had spent time getting in touch with my feelings while I was down with a brain tumor.

What I needed was to stop being in touch with them. I needed a reminder that the monster might not be a very good person, but it was a hell of a weapon. I wasn't Jekyll and Hyde and couldn't be. I had accepted my darkness and it had done well at keeping me alive. Now, I needed to reaccept it and move on, so that the next time the little sixteen year old serial killer stabbed me, I would do more than hold onto her. Killing wasn't required, but a little maiming was in order. It was the psychopathic equivalent of being taken out to the woodshed. I'd gotten my dose. She needed hers.

First though, I needed to suck it up and go to Houston. The CDC was right. I knew a lot about the dissemination of plague. My ability to attract like-minded lunatics was a bonus. Since she had already sent me fan mail, finding me in Houston would probably be an existential moment for her.

Twenty-Six

The ten infected individuals lived in a rundown part of Houston. They and their families were currently being quarantined. The cover story was a nasty strain of flu. This was only going to hold water for so long. It was May and flu season was essentially done.

They also lived near a string of crappy restaurants. Since most of them looked like they served dead rat, there was no chance in hell I would have eaten there, but I didn't belong to this community.

Looking at the situation, I realized I had outdone myself. My paper had suggested poor neighborhoods surrounded by open-air markets and food stalls were exactly the sort of places where infected rats would live. They'd actually thrive there.

Rats were more carriers than infected species. The Norwegian Rats thought to have caused the outbreak in the fourteenth century had shown some immunity to fleas with bubonic plague. It was when these fleas had abandoned the rats for much heartier meals, like dogs, that they would start spreading to humans.

The street was very quiet. It didn't matter that we were two blocks from the quarantine area, it had freaked people out. The restaurants and shops were closed. Every person had just vanished. However, a stray dog was picking through the scraps of a dumpster that catered to three Mexican cantinas.

"Have you started trapping rats and stray animals?" I asked.

"Yes," Peter Corell from the CDC told me. "We started that as soon as the hospital reported their third case."

"It's hard to fathom, really." I looked at the dog. A rat, bigger than a brown rat, ran across the road. The dog growled at it. I didn't know what sort of hybrid rats they had in Texas; it was the Lone Star State after all, and everything was bigger in Texas, but it had seemed like an unusually large one.

"What?" He asked.

"That vacuums and flea baths can get rid of all this," I answered. "Even today, when someone comes down with plague, one of the instructions is vacuum the house, car, and place of business, and dip any pets in flea killer. The disseminator has to be familiar with the area, but does not live in it. You do not release plague-infested fleas in your own neighborhood. You also do not release it where your family works or has a business. So, who else would be familiar with this area?" I continued to stare at the dog. It was now munching on something that had been alive, probably only a day or two ago. "You might grab the mutt and whatever he's eating." I pointed him out to Peter Corell.

"Damn it, where is animal control?" Corell asked.

"There's your disseminator." I pointed as another rat scurried across the road. They didn't seem to mind the presence of myself, Peter, and about seven other people in HAZMAT suits. They were used to a human presence. Most rats were acclimated to some degree to be around people, that's why they were good at surviving in cities. I was fairly sure that acclamation included avoiding people.

"That does seem strange," Peter agreed.

"I'm not an animal behaviorist, but don't rats tend to stay hidden during the day?"

"Cain," Agent Green of the VCU walked up to me. I couldn't remember his first name, but I enjoyed his company. He was Malachi's leash, which gave us a bond that I could neither explain nor break.

"Green," I smiled at the man. He was a few years older, several inches taller, and stocky, and like most of us, there was something wrong with his head. I hadn't figured out exactly what it was yet, but I would, given enough time.

"So, who should we be looking for?" Green asked.

"A woman," I answered. "A deranged woman. Have you seen the rats around here? They are massive. She not only nurtured the bacteria for several years, I think she was hybridizing the rats."

"You are going to have to give me more than that, all women are deranged," Green told me.

"Some more than others, this one is tipping the scales in the straight-jacket department. Talk therapy is not working out her issues."

"Deranged woman who nurtured a virus and rats."

"Bubonic plague is a bacteria, not a virus," Peter Corell offered.

"Doesn't matter, she's still nuttier than a fruitcake," Green answered. "I heard you got stitches in an interesting place."

"No, you may not see the stitches in my ass and not just because I'm wearing a HAZMAT suit. You have a psycho degree. Profile her."

"I do and I've tried. This isn't like the Tylenol Murders or the Bell Tower Sniper. This is new, completely new. Well, not completely new, the Nazis did it, but..." Green trailed off.

"Nazis," I reminded him.

"My thought wasn't about Nazis. Not exactly anyway. What's the rumor? Hitler killed the Jews because he was Jewish and hated it. Our killer may be using *Y. Pestis* because she has the disease or has been affected by the disease," Green said.

"You know the Latin name, but not whether it's a virus or bacteria?" Peter asked.

"I know, I just don't care. It's antibiotic resistant. It might as well be the Hand of God killing these people. We can't really stop it," Green said. "How many cases of plague do we get a year?"

"About two hundred," Peter Corell answered.

"Plague is fairly rare as a killer these days, but it still causes disfigurement," Green said.

"I did not realize you knew so much about plague," I told him.

"Xavier isn't the only medical doctor. I do have a psycho degree, but I got it to work with the VCU. I started out as a med student planning to go into practice working with rare diseases. Plague isn't very common in this area."

"No, it isn't," Peter answered. "Here we are more likely to get tuberculosis, tick-borne illnesses, and Hansen's disease."

"Leprosy is disfiguring," I chimed, "and it still makes people pariahs. That would build a whole lot of anger."

"Hansen's Disease," Peter corrected.

"I know, I just don't care," I mimicked Green. "No one calls it that; if they did, we wouldn't have the term 'avoided like a leper.' Get on your magic machine and start stirring up cases that involve plague or leprosy."

"I'm not a performing monkey," Peter told me.

"Excuse her, she's kind of socially awkward, even among those who are socially awkward," Green apologized. "But she has a point. If I had Hansen's disease and was disfigured, I'd be significantly angry. Considering they are using plague to kill now gives some foundation to the theory that our killer was afflicted by a condition that caused social distancing and disfiguration. Also, while it's rare, they can both have neurological side effects. You might consider checking syphilis as well."

"Adding syphilis would take months," Peter informed us. "It's still really common as an STI."

"What's an STI?"

"Sexually Transmitted Infection," Peter answered.

"What happened to disease?"

"It was changed to sound less terrifying." Peter was opening up his tablet, which was much bigger than my own with more interesting features. I was pretty sure that if I touched it, it would break.

"Sexually transmitted infections should terrify people," I countered the name change. I didn't like when things changed at random.

"The word infection gives a sense of security because infections can be treated and cured. Diseases are far scarier, so people tend to avoid testing, because they don't want to know that they have a disease. Testing and treatment has increased since the change," Green explained to me.

I didn't argue. The name change made sense. It was unsettling to realize that a word change could alter the way an entire species thought about something. It was illogical. Changing from Leprosy to Hansen's disease hadn't removed the stigma of getting it. I remembered the armadillo I had helped earlier. It was possible that in twenty years, I would develop leprosy. I wondered if any of my friends, if they were still alive, would avoid me.

Peter Corell was still doing stuff on his tablet. I looked at the screen. It was a list, a very long list. Leprosy took years, sometimes decades, to become symptomatic. It also took a while to treat, during which time all manner of things could go wrong. My instincts told me that anyone on that list could be a suspect and it probably went back thirty or forty years. It was also likely that while it was a list of people who had caught leprosy in the US and been treated in the US, it also probably contained people that had caught it in other countries and been treated in the US. If there were three hundred or so cases of leprosy every year, the list of suspects was probably anyone on that list.

"How is the werewolf case going?" I asked Green, trying to ignore the never-ending list of suspects that kept popping up in my life.

"Nowhere," Green answered. "Do you have any idea how many people have reported seeing a werewolf in the last month?"

"Yeah, Malachi told me."

"That's not counting the handful of people who are legitimately locked up because they suffer from clinical lycanthropy. If we hadn't found traces of steel in the bite wounds, I might have started believing there was a werewolf in the tristate area of Ohio, Indiana, and Michigan. Your theory about Dogmen helped, but only in the sense that people started telling us stories about people who had gone places and heard unnatural growling attributed to

Dogmen. In Ohio, there's something known as Grassman, which might be Bigfoot or some other primate, or it might be a type of Dogmen or a type of werewolf, or another cryptid. I didn't realize how many people actually believe in cryptids."

"I believe in cryptids," I told him. "Not Bigfoot or aliens, although I have no reason not to believe in them either, but other cryptids."

"That was a confusing and strange statement, Cain," Green told me.

"I am confusing and strange," I told him.

"Do you believe in miracles?" Peter Corell asked.

"I do not disbelieve in them, does that count?" I countered.

"Well, start hoping for one. No one on our list that lives in Texas has a science or medical background. Any other strange diseases you want me to check for?" He asked.

"Damn, I already did this once in Texas. Turned out the killer is just a really smart sixteen year old. Don't suppose that list has the IQs of everyone?"

"No," Peter said.

"IQ only tests one type of intelligence. They are essentially useless, unless you are looking for someone with good math skills, spatial aptitude, and nonlinear based logic," Green pointed out.

"I scored high on one," I answered.

"I believe that, but had you been given different tests, you probably would have scored even higher. Just because a person can do astrophysics doesn't make them brilliant. It makes them a genius. To be brilliant requires more skills than just those tested on an IQ test," Green countered.

"I scored high on all my aptitude tests," I told him.

"This conversation is pointless," Peter interrupted. "For experts, you aren't much help."

"I am not an expert, I'm a trained monkey," I pointed out. "I find serial killers and mass murderers and make them stop. Usually by beating them up. High IQ aside, I'm essentially a weapon to point at bad guys. I can't even remember to wear gloves at crime scenes. This HAZMAT suit is killing me. I'd ditch it if I wasn't terrified of getting plague."

"You wrote the paper that described this exact scenario," Peter Corell pointed out.

"Yeah, when I was seventeen and needed an A. I wrote the first part of the paper for a history class on the Byzantine Empire. I added the second part and edited the first part when I took a class in advanced microbiology and needed an A. I didn't even know it was going to be published until I was in grad school at a totally different college, and I never would have believed anyone would read it, let alone use it to start a biological holocaust. As far as weapons go, plague would not be my first, second, or even last choice. It just worked for different classes and I got lazy," I admitted. "I was taking twenty-four or more hours a semester. Sometimes, I got tired of searching for new material to write papers about."

"Wait, you plagiarized yourself?" Green asked.

"Essentially. I definitely did not cite my other paper as source material," I answered.

"They can take your doctorate for that." Peter joined the conversation.

"I'm a US Marshal chasing serial killers, no one calls me Doctor anyway. They can yank the degree; they cannot yank the knowledge out of my head," I snapped. "Sorry, my wounds hurt. I didn't mean to get cranky. I'm just not the plague expert you think I am. I'm not sure I'm an expert on anything except crime. Even with that, plague is not a good biological weapon. They tried it in the middle ages, catapulting infected corpses over walls to infect the occupants. The only thing it did was lead to new designs for catapults."

"Cain, focus," Green said. "If you were a serial killer, using your paper as a blueprint, what would you do?"

"First, I'd need the bacteria. So, our killer robs a lab at a university and gets it. They have to be associated with the lab to know it even exists. Then I infect some fleas via infected animals, probably rats. Brown rats are the most popular rats for scientific experimentation, but any rodent in the *Rattus* family is essentially a brown rat. These seem to be abnormally large brown rats, so I have bred them in a fashion that makes them bigger. Most likely through superficial identification and mixing them with one of the other fifty members of the *Rattus* family. This takes years. I have to keep a large breeding population of rats, this means I have a society. It might mean I have multiple societies. That takes a lot of room."

"Stop," Peter held up his hand. "You are talking about thousands of rats. It's impossible to keep that many without a laboratory."

"Not necessarily," Green answered. His face was pinched. "When I was a kid, a friend of mine had two rats. His bedroom wall was lined with these tubes. The rats lived in them. There were boxes for nesting, feeding, sleeping, and exercising. We figured it up and there was almost a football field worth of tubing on his wall."

"For two rats?" I asked.

"That's the part that bothers you?" Green asked.

"I just believe they would have been as happy in a large cage," I shrugged.

"Shut up," Green told me. "So, if you have a barn that isn't used for anything, you could end up with miles of tubing. That would be enough to hold thousands of rats and create different colonies, not societies."

"You introduce enough rats at one time to a single area and if they are bigger and more aggressive, they attack the colony already present. The alphas are killed and the new rats take up residence. The new rats are carrying fleas with Y. Pestis. They accept a few newcomers and then the cycle of plague starts," Peter finished.

"And all you need is a barn," Green added.

"Well, I'm glad you guys worked that out. When you find a deranged woman with a barn full of tubing and multiple rat colonies, call me, and I'll beat her up for you." I started walking off. I wasn't sure we had accomplished anything. Well, I knew I hadn't. Green and Peter Corell might have accomplished a lot.

Critical Threshold

Morgan McClure's hand ached. A deep, pulsing ache that went all the way to the bone. The problem was that Morgan didn't have a hand to ache. She started at the stump above where her wrist had once been with disgust, but massaged it anyway. They called them phantom pains. Some kind of neurological memory that happened even though the area that hurt was gone.

Most people would describe Morgan as quiet, shy, and a good worker. She was never late. She never caused problems. She was always the last one to leave at the end of her shift, and she never complained. So, no one noticed that the quiet, shy, hard working girl was seething with hatred.

Morgan hadn't been friends with another person in years, let alone go on a date. Since her parents had died seven years earlier she'd been on her own, completely alone.

The hand was a side effect. Sometime during her childhood, she had contracted leprosy. It had manifested when she was in college. In most cases, the granulomas formed first. Horrid knots under the skin that gave one the skin texture of an ogre.

In Morgan's case, the granulomas had been secondary. Nerve damage had started first. In her left hand to be exact, a condition that would lead to surgeries and the loss of her hand. She'd accidentally let it fall into some grease when she was a fry cook in college. Without being able to feel it, she'd cooked her hand pretty good, resulting in its removal. It was only during her stay in the hospital that the granulomas had started to appear.

She'd been treated for twelve very long months. When the treatment was over, she was still known as a leper. Everyone treated her as such. Her dorm mate had moved out. Her friends stopped talking to her. People just disappeared.

In the years following the treatment and diagnosis, the stigma stood. It was hard to lie all the

314

time about the scars and the missing hand. Telling people made them take steps away from her.

She'd become bitter. She'd shut herself in. Her only pleasure was her job. Most people didn't think working for the city of Houston as a rodent exterminator was a decent lifestyle choice. It suited Morgan though.

It was going to allow her to get revenge on society. As a student, she'd come across a paper discussing how antibiotic resistant bubonic plague would be devastating to a modern city. The author had used the Justinian Plague that hit Constantinople as the model for dissemination.

It was working. Not as fast as the author of the paper had thought it would. Or Morgan, but it was working. She was starting to find dead cats and dogs along her route. More than could be naturally explained. A few had showed signs of infection. She had dutifully wrapped them in plastic before picking them up.

As the infected rat population spread through the poor and urban areas, it would move from rats to pets and from pets to people. At least, according to the model. Morgan hadn't heard of any infected people yet, but she was sure it was coming. The work had shown enough promise that she had taken a large number of infected rats to Dallas a few nights earlier and released them.

The world had been cruel to her. She had every right to be cruel back. However, she wasn't totally heartless. She'd thanked the author of the paper by sending her a flash frozen squirrel from her initial tests.

Morgan had planned to be a zoologist before her leprosy activated. She'd been a student at a large, east coast university with plans to get the hell away from Texas. She'd wanted to get her degree and go to work for a large zoo, where she could be a veterinarian. An armadillo had squashed those dreams. An armadillo from ten years before. One that had wandered into her house when she was a child. Her parents had considered it an act of God. She thought it was Mother Nature being a bitch.

Then the world had turned on her. If it was an act of God, as her parents had proclaimed, God was an asshole. His obvious disregard for her happiness and her quality of life proved it.

However, she'd get back at both Mother Nature and God too. Some of the rats had been released near an animal sanctuary. Others were released near churches; there were a lot of those in Texas.

Tonight, she'd hit the next largest town in Texas. San Antonio was a long drive, but well worth it. After that, she'd hit Austin, and maybe target the University of Texas specifically. Having the outbreak start there would be poetic.

She massaged the stump a little more and then added the prosthetic hand. The hand had been expensive, but she had wanted it to look natural. As natural as possible anyway. People still had no desire to touch it, but she understood. There were days when she didn't want to touch it.

With approximately three hundred rats in the back of her truck, Morgan set off. The drive to San Antonio was right at three hours. Thankfully, the tarp and cab of the truck would provide her with some protection. At some point, she knew she would be infected with the deadly strain of plague. Her goal was to let it loose in the major cities of Texas first.

317

As she neared San Antonio, the radio gave an update on a manhunt being conducted by the US Marshals Service. A teenaged girl, named Jessica Blanks was wanted by authorities in connection with murder. The girl was five feet tall, blue eyes, light brown hair, and weighed ninety pounds.

How anyone that small could commit murder was beyond Morgan's comprehension. Her victim must have been very small. Maybe she had killed a child in an episode of "Babysitter Gone Really Bad." The thought made Morgan smile. They would have a lot more problems than some deranged babysitter soon enough. Her work in Houston was proving that it took weeks, but they were weeks well spent.

Morgan had mapped out the area weeks ago using animal control data from the city. The soft underbelly of San Antonio was easy to find, if you followed the rat populations. They were drawn to areas where there were lots of restaurants, or where the poor were clustered. She understood why too. The poor didn't have the money to exterminate them. Most had trouble keeping mousetraps, let alone a rattrap in the house.

However, it was the business district that worked best. The rats infected stray dogs and cats, who visited the same dumpsters looking for food. The strays then infected pets and other animals. From there, it was just a waiting game before some idiot who forgot to flea dip their pet got infected. No one really understood how strays interacted with pets. It would have been better in St. Louis, Missouri, and Los Angeles, California.

Both of those cities had packs of strays that roamed the streets due to ineffective animal control measures. As a matter of fact, a young girl had recently been torn to shreds by a pack of stray dogs in St. Louis. It had made the national news because it was the third attack in as many months.

She parked in an alley behind a group of restaurants. One proclaimed to have the best tacos in Texas. She doubted this was true. Everyone claimed to have the best tacos in Texas.

She shut off the lights of her truck and waited. It was after two a.m. If her vehicle was spotted, there would be questions, but she had to be sure.

After ten minutes or so, sitting in the truck, she saw the first rat. It came out of a hole in the sidewalk, right under the place that proclaimed to have the best tacos in Texas. She smiled. The tacos were going to get a little more interesting.

She put on her big, heavy leather gloves. They were supposed to be able to protect her from vicious dogs, feral cats, feisty armadillos, and determined rats. They had always done their job in the past.

Tonight was no different. She pulled the cages of rats out of the bed and set them near the dumpsters. The rat population of the area went back into hiding. They would fight to keep their homes free of the interlopers. This was expected. Rats were social, but territorial.

The door went up and the first group of about fifty rats was released into the alleyway. They searched for places to hide. A group of them headed towards the hole in the sidewalk, where she had seen the other pop up from earlier.

The residents of the hole chased the intruders out. The new rats cowered in the alleyway for a moment. She opened the door to another cage, then a third, then all seven of them. Now, outnumbered, the San Antonio rats were the ones fleeing their secure tunnels. A new hierarchy was being established. It was social Darwinism in action.

Her rats had not been humanized, but they had been given plenty of food and kept in darkness most of the time. They were bigger than their San Antonio cousins based on how they had been raised. Also, while most rats living in the darkness of cities were brown rats, her rats had a little genetic boost. She'd introduced two other species of rats to the genetic group, increasing their heartiness and genetic diversity.

She hadn't intended to make a larger rat. She had really just wanted to increase the survivability of them, but the law of unintended consequences had kicked in, as it always does when dealing with biology, and the rats had become somewhat larger than the plain brown rat.

Once they established dominance in this area, they would allow the displaced rats back into the group. Not all of them, the alpha would be killed, but the others would be allowed to return to their homes. Almost all of them would begin carrying fleas infected with antibiotic resistance bubonic plague.

The order of nature was amazing to watch. The displaced rats were already searching for new homes. A few of the larger, more aggressive males were attempting to regain control. The larger, infested rats were winning. Tomorrow, someone would be cleaning up rat carcasses, unless some enterprising animals came along and scavenged their bodies.

In an area like this, it was very probable that a few cats or dogs would feed on the dead rats. It would be a good starting place for the plague to jump to its next host. The chain had already begun with a simple little fight for dominance.

Morgan packed the cages up. She got in her truck and headed east, back to Houston. It was going to be a good day, even if she did go to work exhausted.

Disappearing

Jess was following the highway. She was headed east, away from the lights and noise, and papers and news stations broadcasting her face. It was unimaginable that a stupid cop had stopped her. Her life was in freefall. Her secret was out. There was no way it couldn't be, not after killing the Marshal.

It was a regrettable setback, but Jess had resources. She had access to her brother's account. She had her sister's identification. They could nearly pass as twins. She'd buy a ticket in her sister's name and head to Mexico. Once in Mexico, she'd hop a flight to an Asian country. She'd teach English or something. There was always work for English teachers in Asia. Her sister had done a year abroad, teaching English in Thailand. She had loved it. Jess could do that. Her sister's credentials would get her into the country and get her a job.

Unfortunately, she'd been on the move for over a day. Her legs were starting to get sore. She wanted to sit down, but if she stopped, she'd get caught. She'd stayed off the highways and busy streets because of this. Until now.

Jess felt a growing sense of urgency. She had to get to a big city. She had to get somewhere and blend in. Her feet took her to the interstate. It was dangerous walking the interstate. Someone might recognize her.

A truck slowed down, its headlights illuminating her body, making her shadow grow tall on the ground in front of her. The truck got back on the highway. It crawled past her. She forced herself not to look up. It pulled in front of her and stopped on the shoulder again.

Jess did look up now. A woman was hanging out the driver's window. She had a scar on her face that the shadows didn't hide, only accentuated.

"Want a ride?" She asked Jess. Jess thought for a moment. She still had the baton she'd taken off the Marshal. While she was quite a bit older than

Jess, Jess was certain that she could kill her if the need arose. Her body sighed at the thought of a ride, even if it was just twenty miles.

"Thanks," Jess picked up her pace and jumped into the passenger's side of the truck. The woman was in her early thirties or so. She needed a manicure and some make-up, but she felt non-threatening. She was also missing a hand. The prosthetic didn't grip the steering wheel quite right.

"My name's Morgan," the woman said.

"Becky," Jess lied, "Becky Childs."

"Nice to meet you, Becky. What on earth are you doing out here at this time of night?" Morgan pulled back onto the highway.

"Getting away," Jess sized the woman up. If she got too nosy, she'd just kill her and take the truck. She could hide the body off the highway. Jess would be in Thailand before they found her.

"I understand," Morgan agreed.

Morgan stopped talking. The truck had a strange smell. A stench that Jess couldn't identify. It wasn't pleasant, but it wasn't entirely unpleasant either. Of course, her sense of smell had never been very good. It affected her sense of taste as well. The

325

doctor said it was because the olfactory system wasn't completely developed. He didn't know why, but said he'd seen it a few times in other patients. There was nothing to be done about it.

Jess's body wanted to drift off to sleep. Her brain was fighting to keep it awake. She would be in trouble if she fell asleep and this woman turned out to be crazy.

"So, are you just going to admit who you really are?" Morgan asked as they had driven a while. "And where you plan to go?"

"What?" Jess was instantly awake.

"You're the girl from the news, I don't remember the name they gave, but out of San Marcos. The one wanted for murder."

"No, I'm not," Jess said sternly.

"Oh please," Morgan gave a quick laugh. "I'm not going to turn you in. I don't care if there is a person or two less in this world because of you. I'm headed to Houston. You can ride the whole way, if you're headed that far."

"Who are you?" Jess asked, her defenses up.

"Morgan McClure, spreader of bubonic plague. I was in San Antonio tonight releasing infected rats. It's probably a good thing you got out of there. In a few weeks, the town will be dealing with an epidemic. Actually, most of Texas will be dealing with one."

"Uh huh," Jess nodded. This woman was obviously crazy. Not your garden variety crazy either, but the type that earned straightjackets and electroshock therapy. "Jess Blanks, serial killer of worthless teenagers." Jess told her. The label felt good. It felt right. Her hand found the baton. She carefully pulled it from her pocket.

"Serial killer, nice, so much better than a babysitter gone mad. The news hasn't announced they suspect you of being a serial killer. In a few months or so, they'll be denouncing me as a mass murderer, but they won't really get it. They did it to themselves. A little kindness could have prevented all of this. Jess, the Serial Killer, I recommend you get as far from Texas as you possibly can. Reinvent yourself as a serial killer somewhere colder, like Maine or Alaska. Plague spreads slower in colder climates according to research I've done."

"Ok," Jess agreed. This woman was definitely crazy. Jess looked around. It would probably be better to kill the woman and take the truck. Jess was convinced the woman wouldn't turn her in, but she didn't need this kind of trouble. She suddenly whipped out the baton and struck Morgan McClure with it.

"Ouch! What the fuck!" Morgan swerved across the highway. Jess hadn't thought it through all the way. Attacking Morgan, who currently controlled the vehicle that was rocketing down the highway, was probably not her best-laid plan. Jess swung at Morgan again while grabbing the wheel. The speed of the vehicle was dropping. Morgan slumped against the driver's window. Jess guided the car onto the shoulder. There wasn't another car in sight.

Jess had to climb onto Morgan's lap to get the truck to a stop. There was a small road off to the side. Jess pushed the seat back to get to the pedals. She'd driven sitting on her dad's lap when she was younger, but this was completely different. She flipped on the flashers as the truck crept along.

The turn was difficult to make. The dead woman's feet were getting in Jess's way and she didn't have enough room to maneuver her elbows. The truck bounced across the ditch of the opposite lane as they entered the small road. She drove about forty feet down the gravel before stopping the truck again. There were cows and thick underbrush here, nothing else. It was as good a place as any to ditch Morgan's body.

Jess opened the driver's side door and Morgan's body slipped from behind her. With the dead woman half in and half out of the truck, Jess climbed out. The lap harness of the seat belt had captured Morgan's body and kept her suspended. Jess had missed it earlier because, despite it being buckled, the shoulder harness was behind Morgan's body. Jess reached to unbuckle it.

Morgan's eyes flew open. The baton that Jess had forgotten about in her scramble to control the truck was in Morgan's hand. The older woman brought the baton down on the sixteen year-old. The belt unfastened and they both fell to the ground, Morgan on top of Jess. Jess had already done this. She had some bruises from it. She knew how much the baton hurt. She raised her arm to block the blow. The baton connected with the broken limb, and the bone that had mesmerized Jess on the volleyball court pierced through the skin.

Like with the Marshal, Jess realized she was in trouble. However, she'd had a knife then. She didn't have one now. She had nothing to help her attack or defend. The baton came down on her again, forcing the air from her lungs. Her bones cracked under the force. Her ribs felt like they were on fire. Her lungs felt as if she were drowning.

Jess struggled to push Morgan off of her. She tried to immobilize Morgan like the Marshal had done to her, but with only one hand, the bigger woman who wielded the baton was too much for her to handle. The baton connected with Jess's knee. The pain was excruciating. It seared itself into her brain, making it hard to think.

Never had she experienced anything like this. The pain, the helplessness, they worked against her. The rage that she had found when killing Sabrina Reeves and Simon Westbrook wouldn't come to her. Instead, her heartbeat picked up. Her breathing became labored.

The baton hit her midsection. There was instant pressure in her abdomen. She hadn't even noticed Morgan moving. The pressure was a bad sign. The baton had ruptured something. Jess could feel it, pushing on her insides, making it hard to inflate her lungs. She wet herself and could do nothing about it. She stared at Morgan.

Morgan grinned. The look of malice and joy were ghoulish in the light from the cab of the truck. Jess realized she was dying. This was not how it was supposed to work, damn it. She was supposed to be the killer, not the crazy woman who spoke of rats and had only one hand.

She must have been more injured by the Marshal than she thought. Coupled with the walking, she hadn't been at her best. She was going to die, staring up at Morgan McClure and thinking of rats. She would not give her killer that satisfaction.

Jess tilted her head up. Her stomach was now churning. Thankfully, it was empty. Her gaze found stars. The sky overhead was beautiful. It would have been a good night to climb up onto Shawn's roof and look through his telescope, but Shawn was dead. She had made sure of that. She'd done it for the right reasons. Becky was never going to like him. There was no need for him to suffer that heartbreak for the rest of his life.

The moon was sinking below the horizon, but it was still bright. In a few days, it would be full. Pity, she was going to miss it. She loved full moons. There was a pinprick of pain on her arm, like she'd just been bitten by a mosquito or something. She looked at the area. It was beginning to swell. Maybe it was a chigger or flea.

Her body spasmed, hard. The pain was immense. Then it stopped. There was no pain. There were no reminders of her body at all. Then there was no thought. Her eyes took on the vacant stare that belongs to the dead.

Twenty-Seven

My phone was ringing. Darkness still showed through the slit of curtain in my hotel room, so it wasn't good news. I considered not answering it. I had also considered sleeping in my HAZMAT suit, but was told that would send the wrong message. So, I had the maids vacuum my room twice before I would take my suit off. Peter Corell was not happy with me. I understood. It was really hard to be my boss.

For Peter Corell, it was worse, because I didn't consider him my boss. He did. This was never a good situation for the person who was theoretically in charge. Malachi had tried to smooth things over, but it hadn't worked.

My phone stopped ringing. I closed my eyes. It started ringing again.

"It's dark out. You have bad news. Can't it wait until the sun is up?" I said without looking to see who was calling.

"No," Gabriel told me. "You are closer to Houston than we are. Lucas and I are on the way, but someone has reportedly found and killed Jessica Blanks. I need you and Xavier there, immediately."

"Vigilantism?" I was tired of vigilantes. This probably had something to do with my family.

"Knowing Blanks was desperate, there's a good chance the victim's claim of self-defense is true. I want someone who deals with serial killers all the time to check it out. That is you and Xavier."

"And Malachi," I added.

"I'm not sending Malachi to talk to a woman who might be a victim. I want a statement, not a transcript that reads like Greek because huge chunks are omitted."

"Why would huge parts be omitted?" I asked.

"It's Malachi Blake," Gabriel hung up on me.

My phone flashed 4:32 a.m. before the screen went black. I really hoped that Jessica Blanks wasn't dead. I had questions for the psychopath, like how the hell did she manage to melt the bodies found in the shed. I knew her motives, psychopaths really could hyper focus after a kill. The dopamine flooding their brains made them feel euphoric and that euphoria could be transferred. If she studied her behind off for an exam while in the euphoric state, she'd get a small secondary rush when she got her exam back with an A on it.

Her method met her needs, clean kills that boosted her endorphins and dopamine was all she wanted. Until Sabrina Reeves. That had been messy. That had been brutal. That had been personal. Just like Simon Westbrook. There was no doubt that Jessica Blanks had picked Simon Westbrook to fulfill some role in her life. His sleeping around and ignoring her didn't mesh with her fantasy. She'd killed Sabrina first and realized that only solved part of the problem. Her disappointment was still up. So she had killed Simon Westbrook.

However, that left Shawn. I wasn't sure how Shawn fit into the picture. He was a friend, not a threat. His role in her life was fairly concrete. They'd been friends since childhood. He wasn't Becky, but he wasn't chopped liver either. Why had she killed Shawn?

Xavier quietly knocked on my door as I was trying to put on my shoes. It hurt. A dull ache ran the length of my body. If the government hadn't decided they needed me, I'd be holed up somewhere, recuperating. I was getting old from all the beatings, stabbings, and shootings. I was still recovering from my tumor, not the surgery, but the actual tumor. It had caused damage that I couldn't explain, like my inability just to ignore the pain.

I got up and let him in. He frowned at me as I sat back down on the bed. I reached for my shoe again.

"Stop," Xavier's voice was soft. He shut the door. "We don't want the vultures circling. Let me."

"Vultures circling?" I raised an eyebrow as he reached for my shoe.

"The moment you start showing weakness, the whack jobs that follow you around are going to move in to pick the carcass clean. Your carcass. I haven't said anything, but you are not at one hundred percent yet. I see it once in a while, in your face. Without your sanity mask, it's amazing what a person who knows you can learn. You can't ignore the pain yet, not like you used to. You aren't completely distancing yourself, like you used to. I think it will come back, but it isn't here yet. You bend over to put on your shoes and you're going to have to force yourself not to walk favoring one side. I put on your shoes and there's less of a chance of that leaning gait."

"Do the others know?"

"No, but they haven't been watching you like I have. They've been trying to assess your mental state, which seems to be fine. I've been assessing your physical state and it's still playing catch up with the mental one."

"One could argue that my mental and physical state are the same in this situation."

"They could, but they would be wrong. I've been around you long enough to realize that some of our perceived ideas of psychopaths and sociopaths is wrong. I realized some time ago that the problem with our understanding of the conditions comes from the mouths of those that have it. Unfortunately, those people are very good liars. You included. Just because you try not to lie, doesn't mean you don't withhold the truth at times. Lucas has come to the same conclusion. All those years of research have become practically meaningless. That's why when we deal with the real thing, Lucas asks you about psychological analysis."

"Sometimes, I think about telling you guys what really goes on in my head and then I stop myself. Like I'm breaking some unwritten rule that real people cannot know the whole truth."

"I agree with that. I think if the general public were actually to get all the data on psychopaths and sociopaths, they would panic. Myself included. It doesn't matter how much we study, we cannot fully understand them. That's why we have you and the FBI has Malachi." Xavier finished my shoes. "Now, let's go talk to Morgan McClure and figure out what happened. I had questions for Jessica Blanks, like the melted bodies, so I'm hoping she's just injured and not dead."

"Me too."

We bought two Mountain Dews from the machine on our way out. My brain functioned better with caffeine. So did Xavier's and there wasn't coffee made in the lobby for him to grab a cup. It was unusual for him to drink soda, but addicts were addicts, even if it meant switching things up.

The drive was quiet. Xavier, despite his strange qualities, was a decent guy. There were moments when he showed true kindness.
Considering all the death, gore, blood, and evil that surrounded us all the time, it was interesting to watch the men on my team hold it together.

Swirling lights directed us to the scene. It wasn't on the highway. It was on some little gravel road off the interstate. A woman sat in the back of an ambulance. Blood had dried on her face. Her hair was matted. She looked rough.

On the ground was a body under a sheet. Blood had soaked through the sheet. The outline was small enough to be that of Jessica Blanks.

We parked and flashed our badges. Xavier went to talk to the victim. I lifted up the sheet. Karma had come to call on Jessica. She'd been beaten to death. My answers were under the sheet with her though. There would be no explanation on why she killed Shawn. I would never know how she made the shed so humid her victims had melted.

"Hey, Cain," Xavier yelled to me. I stood up. My baton was in an evidence bag on the hood of a squad car.

"That's mine, I want it back," I told an officer.

"It's evidence, Marshal," he told me. I sighed. I had known that, but I still wanted it back.

"Ms. McClure, this is US Marshal Aislinn Cain. She's going to stand here with you for a few minutes, while I check on some things." I didn't frown, although, I really wanted to. I wasn't good with victims and Xavier knew it.

"Dr. Cain," she nodded at me. It obviously hurt. I stared at her. There was a deep-pitted scar on her face. She was missing her left hand. There were insect bites on her arm, and she had called me Doctor, not Marshal.

"So, what do you do for a living, Ms. McClure?" I asked.

"I work for the City of Houston," she answered.

"Ah, government work." I stopped looking at her and started looking into the dawning sun. The horizon was turning orange. "What type of work for the city?"

"I'm an exterminator," she shrugged.

"They didn't give you mosquito repellent while you waited?" I pointed to her arms.

"Um, no, I didn't realize I had been bitten."

"Shock, I'm sure. It happens after something like this."

"Ok," Xavier came back, "I had to call some colleagues. Green, Blake and Corell are on their way." Xavier had noticed them too. Clichés aside, psychopaths really did attract other psychopaths. I didn't understand it, I just knew it happened, often. It was how serial killing teams and couples found each other. They were just drawn together. I didn't need to hear Morgan McClure's sob story about doing a good deed. She was just as crazy as Jessica Blanks was. Jessica's injuries proved it. Somehow, the woman had overpowered the girl and killed her, and Xavier was right, we were all great liars. It was easy to see how the police had bought her story of self-defense and luck. I knew the three men were not on their way to our location, they were on their way to Morgan McClure's house to see if she was our disseminator. Judging by the fleabites and the scars, she was.

"How long ago did you get diagnosed with Hansen's Disease?" Xavier suddenly ambushed Morgan McClure.

341

"Um, while I was in college, it's been a while." She looked at him. "How did you know?"

"The scar and missing hand," I told her. "We were thinking it might have been plague, but judging by how angry someone would have to be and how plague isn't really common in Texas, leprosy was the next best thing. I did not appreciate the dead squirrel."

"I don't know what you're talking about." Morgan's demeanor changed.

"You called me Doctor Cain, not Marshal Cain. Even those that know I'm a doctor, do not use the title. That plus the fleabites on your arms, tells me that you sent me the infected squirrel. Very few people would pick up a hitchhiker at this time of morning, let alone survive an attack by a psychopath while driving. The entire situation tells me you're angry, very angry, and rightfully so. Most people still treat Hansen's Disease patients like lepers, literally. You were probably a highly functioning psychopath before Hansen's. Hansen's made you bitter and angry. Now, you're trying to start a biological holocaust." I didn't know where to put the handcuffs. She would have slipped out of one of them and while

I had never been punched in the face by a stump, I was sure it would hurt.

Twenty-Eight

Morgan McClure sprang at me from the ambulance. Her hand latched onto my hair. Her other arm encircled my neck. Her body hung from mine. The attack was sudden and I hadn't been ready for it. I stumbled backwards, trying to keep my balance as she wrapped her legs around me.

Her teeth suddenly sank into my face. The calm washed over me. Her movements appeared in slow motion. My eyes searched for a weapon.

I grabbed at her, found her hair and started pulling. I needed to put some separation between us. I swiveled and rammed her body into the grill of her truck. Officers were drawing weapons. Xavier was shouting orders for them to hold their fire.

I slammed her into the grill again. Her legs unwrapped this time and she lost her grip. I took the moment to grab her. My leg took her feet out from under her, as we landed together in a heap, with me on top. She attempted to get up. Her body moved in an effort to buck me off.

My knee found her spine and held her to the ground. Still, she squirmed and twisted. I pulled my Taser. The cartridge spot was still empty. I hadn't replaced it. I could use it as a stun gun, but the truth was, I didn't feel much like getting Tasered. The output was high enough that it would travel through both our bodies and I was still healing. Being Tasered would put me at a disadvantage.

She twisted and hit my leg with something. The pain was immediate. Blood blossomed through my jeans. It dripped from her hand. A chunk of glass was sticking out of the wound.

My anger spilled over, turning into rage. I let her roll, let her think she had the upper hand. Once she was on her back, I grabbed hold of her shirt. My hand twisted the fabric around itself. She punched the glass shard with her stump. The sound of bone hitting glass seemed very loud. Her heart was racing. I could feel it jackhammering against my hand, even through the knotted fabric. I wanted to break her neck. The urge was so strong, it took every ounce of control not to do it. I stood up, bringing her with me using the shirt.

"Do something with her," I told an officer standing close to me. He slipped a handcuff over the wrist with a hand, but like me, he wasn't sure what else to do. There should have been a manual or something about cuffing handless suspects.

I let go. Her momentum carried both her and the officer to the ground. I turned to see Xavier. His eyes were wide. His mouth opened. There was a muffled popping noise. Someone screamed. Weapons were being raised. I turned back around. She was getting to her feet. I charged her, catching her in the stomach. She scrambled backwards to stay upright as my body shoved her backwards. The butt of the gun hit my shoulder. It didn't hurt. My brain ignored it.

She didn't hit me a second time, she shot me. The bullet entered near my shoulder and exited near my collarbone. It hit the pavement, leaving a mark. I stood up and pulled her into me, twisting her arm as I did. The bones snapped, the sound echoed.

My hand grabbed the knife on my shoulder holster. The blade dug deep into her flesh. I pulled it out and stabbed her a second time. The blade hit bone. I jerked it out. The tip was missing. I stabbed her again, this time lower. Instead of jerking it out, I pressed hard and used my body to pull it along the soft flesh of her abdomen.

"Holy shit!" Someone shouted.

I yanked the knife out. Morgan McClure looked shocked. Her eyes were wide. Her mouth opened and closed, but no sound came out. Her face paled. I stepped back, kicking stuff off my shoe as I did.

Her face turned downwards. She stared at her eviscerated abdomen. Her hand tried to hold stuff in the gaping wound. Slowly, she sank to her knees. I stood a few feet away and watched. Someone stepped in and tried to help her. Xavier grabbed hold of me, turning me away from the scene.

"Well, I think you might be physically normal again," he said. I wanted to sit down and he wouldn't let me. He kept me standing. "You are going to need a hospital bed in a quarantined room."

"Why?" I snapped at him.

"She might have been in the early stages of infection. Her blood could have infected you," he told me. "I'll make sure they give you your tablet and phone."

"I hate hospitals."

"I know," Xavier told me. "The stitches in your backside need to be redone. That glass shard is in an artery, we can't pull it out. Your side is bleeding, and you don't care about any of it, do you? Do you even feel it?"

"Not really," I looked at my leg. My jeans were soaked. Blood dripped from the hem. My shoes were also covered, but that wasn't mine.

"When that goes away, you are going to be in some serious pain," Xavier warned me.

"If it doesn't go away?" I asked.

"We'll have to deal with that." Xavier looked at me. "You do know what you did, right?"

"Her intestines are on my shoes. I wanted to break her neck, but I didn't. I think that should win me some points."

"Jesus Christ," Gabriel's voice drifted on the night air.

"She shot a cop, she shot me, and I was defending myself," I immediately started defending myself.

"Yeah, I got that from the officers that let me in. Are you okay?" Gabriel asked.

I shrugged.

"Are you okay?" He spoke slowly and loudly, as though I was deaf.

"I have been shot, stabbed twice, and beaten with my own baton all in the space of three days. We have two dead killers. We have questions with no answers, and there is yucky stuff on my shoes," I also spoke slowly and loudly. "What part of this am I supposed to be okay with?"

The calm was retreating. I was starting to feel queasy. My stomach churned. It was the stuff on my shoes. I started pushing on the heel with my other shoe, determined to get them off.

"Let's get you to the hospital," a paramedic told me. He looked at my feet. "I'll take them off inside."

The paramedic did indeed take off my shoes and shove them in a HAZMAT bag. I got all my old stitches taken out and new stitches put in. My face didn't need any. I was kind of thankful for that. My face had a few scars, but not like the rest of me, and then I was shoved in a hospital room with an air lock and too many windows.

For six days, I sat in my air locked room with its own special ventilation system. There was a TV. There was a chair. There was a table. My meals were given to me by people in HAZMAT suits. The doctor that visited wore a HAZMAT suit. The nurses wore suits. No one was allowed to visit.

I read just over a hundred books in six days, none of them about crime, which was surprising. All of them were about the paranormal or clinical lycanthropy. On the fifth day, I got a text from Green. My tip about the full moon had worked out. Since I had killed Morgan McClure, they had returned to Indiana, Ohio, and Michigan to search for their serial killer. On the second night of the full moon, they had caught some idiot in a suit made entirely from wolf pelts stalking some girl. He was already claiming insanity.

The CDC had found almost two miles of tubes in Morgan McClure's outbuilding. It was an enclosed carport that looked like a normal shed. They also found more rats. Inside the tubes, running around like crazy, as well as in Dallas and San Antonio. There were no reported cases of plague yet in those cities, but they were watching.

The strain of plague turned out not to be as antibiotic resistant as originally thought. A mixture of doxycycline and ciprofloxacin was effective. However, both were required and it didn't hurt to add some streptomycin in the first twenty-four hours.

Not a single person had died. The cities with the infected fleas had called in the National Guard to help them exterminate the vermin. All stray dogs and cats were being rounded up. Emergency flea dip centers were opened by the Humane Society of Texas where people could get their pets dipped for free. Even the wildlife was receiving treatment.

After six days, I was still symptom free. I had not caught the plague. This made me feel pretty good about the outcome. I still had questions without answers, but there was always going to be that possibility.

Epilogue

My mother and my mutant puppy greeted me when I arrived home. Obviously, they had missed me. The puppy was exceptionally happy about seeing me. So much so, that he peed on me. I gave him to my mother.

"You were on the news. They are calling you a hero," my mother informed me as she put the puppy in the backyard.

"Why?" I asked.

"You stopped an epidemic." She walked into the kitchen and washed her hands. "They glossed over the fact that you killed someone to do it."

"Mom, if you want to live here..." I started.

"I'm not judging. I'm just saying that the news pretty much ignored that. I thought it was big of them. Your talk with the Chadwicks has had some unexpected consequences. They are trying to sue you."

"Oh, really." I pulled out my phone. My intent was to call Franklin and see how his investigation was going. He didn't answer, so I left a message, including the new information regarding a lawsuit.

"I'm making roast for dinner. Elle and Cassie are coming over."

"What about my nephew?" His name had escaped me. I would have to work on that.

"He is at camp already," my mother chided me.

"Camp? Doesn't he have school?"

"They ended while you were in quarantine. He left the next day for smart kids' camp."

"Oh, is he smart?"

"Both of them are very bright. You should take some interest." My mother came into the living room. "It's good to have you home, honey."

I wouldn't admit it, but it was good to be home, even if it did include a leaky puppy and my mother.

A Note About The Series

For seven books, I have argued that sociopaths and psychopaths do not have much emotional depth. This is true and also, untrue.

Since the first diagnosis of the condition, researchers have mostly relied upon the sociopaths and psychopaths themselves to explain it. As Ted Bundy said, he felt nothing, all the time. The problem with that is, both are known as adept liars. Bundy was once in love, proving that he had to feel something. So how much of our understanding is based upon the lies?

It turns out, quite a bit. Groundbreaking research was published in 2006 by Danish researchers. They used a control group, a group of psychopaths, and a group of sociopaths in their study and tested them in three areas: empathy, the ability to recognize emotions, and their brain structures.

In the first test, they hooked everyone up to a brainwave monitor and showed all three groups a video of a person getting their hand smacked with a ruler. The control group (normal people) reacted with the proper empathy, their brain waves registering they felt the pain experienced by the person in the video. The psychopaths and sociopaths did not.

The group was then asked to "feel what the person in the video was feeling." The control group actually over empathized. Their brain waves reporting that they not only understood pain was involved, but actually had been struck themselves. Surprisingly, the brain waves of psychopaths showed they were able to empathize when asked to do so. Oddly, the sociopaths tended to laugh when asked to empathize.

In the second test, everyone was shown pictures and asked to identify what the person was feeling. Sociopaths and the control group did very well. Psychopaths were unable to identify fear. As one poetically put it, "I don't know that emotion, but it's the same look people get when I stab them."

Surprised by how well the sociopaths did, they retested the subjects with a real person in a one-on-one situation. The results were confusing. Psychopaths were still unable to recognize fear, but the sociopaths failed the test miserably. Often they mistook sadness and pain as happiness when they were face-to-face.

The third test did indeed find structural differences in the brain of both psychopaths and sociopaths. Psychopaths have underdeveloped olfactory systems, resulting in a poor sense of taste and smell. They have an excessive number of dopamine receptors, which is where people experience pleasure. They have fewer receptors for pain, so they actually don't feel it like a normal person. Sociopaths were found to have higher baselines of epinephrine and norepinephrine. They also had fewer pain receptors. And for some reason, while their olfactory system was fine, they had trouble distinguishing colors of similar hues when they were near each other.

What this means: Psychopaths do not feel fear, do not recognize fear and actually do have emotions. Sociopaths are not capable of empathizing and have trouble with interpersonal relationships because their brains become confused by emotions when they are dealing with a real person.

The real telling piece of information, the one that brought about this study, was given to the world by a serial killer named Andrei Chikatilo. He told doctors he "could feel, [he] just choose not to, it was something [he] could control, like a switch, turning [his] emotions on and off to meet the requirements of the situation."

This has led to a better understanding of psychopaths such as John Wayne Gacy, who entertained hospitalized children and then killed an unknown amount of young men. It also reminds us that Ted Bundy, who provided the basis for most of understanding of the modern day sociopath and psychopath, was lying to us.

About the Author

I've been writing for over two decades and before that, I was creating my own bedtime stories to tell myself. I penned my first short story at the ripe old age of eight. It was a fable about how the raccoon got its eye-mask and was roughly three pages of handwritten, eight year old scrawl. My mother still has it, and occasionally I still dig it out and admire it.

When I got my first computer, I took all my handwritten stories and typed them in. Afterwards, I tossed the originals. In my early twenties, I had a bit of a writer's meltdown and deleted everything. So, with the exception of the story about the raccoon, I actually have none of my writings from before I was 23. Which is sad, because I had a half dozen other novels and well over two hundred short stories. It has all been offered up to the computer and writing gods as a sacrifice and show of humility or some such nonsense that makes me feel less like an idiot about it.

I have been offered contracts with publishing houses in the past and always turned them down. Now that I have experimented with being an Indie Author, I really like it and I'm really glad I turned them down. However, if you had asked me this in the early years of 2000, I would have told you that I was an idiot (and it was a huge contributing factor to my deleting all my work).

When I'm not writing, I play in a steel-tip dart league and enjoy going to dart tournaments. I enjoy renaissance festivals and sanitized pirates who sing sea shanties. My appetite for reading is ferocious and I consume two to three books a week as well as writing my own. Aside from introducing me to darts, my Significant Other has introduced me to camping, which I, surprisingly, enjoy. We can often be found in the summer at Mark Twain Lake in Missouri, where his parents own a campground.

I am a native of Columbia, Missouri, which I will probably call home for the rest of my life; but I love to travel. Day trips, week trips, vacations on other continents, wherever the path takes me is where I want to be and I'm hoping to be able to travel more in the future.

http://www.facebook.com/hadenajames

hadenajames.wordpress.com

@hadenajames

Newsletter